Gage was kidnapped years ago and taken far from his home in America. He was sold into sexual slavery to the owner of a mining operation in Russia, but soon found himself being used to reward the miners for their productivity. He dreams of escape every day. He is finally rescued by a mysterious man who seems to be able to do magic. He has an unusual reaction to his emancipators and is taken to their camp in Romania. The coven master appears and offers him a job opportunity, but Gage turns out to be something the warlocks have never encountered before. The coven master tests him and Gage knows that he has met his true Master. Gage is torn between seeing his family for the first time in years or staying with the man of his dreams. And deep inside he knows that he still wants revenge . . .

The Mystic Master
Copyright © 2019 Crawford Rhine
ISBN: 978-1-4874-2544-9
Cover art by Angela Waters

Published by eXtasy Books Inc or
Devine Destinies, an imprint of eXtasy Books Inc

Look for us online at:
www.eXtasybooks.com or www.devinedestinies.com

THE MYSTIC MASTER
ROMANIAN CHRONICLES BOOK 4

BY

CRAWFORD RHINE

CHAPTER ONE

Part of a journal written by the sexual slave, Drotik, on the first of April two thousand and nineteen, in English.

Today is different.

I feel like something is going to happen to me today. Something different. Something positive.

There is a tingling coming from inside me that I have never felt before. It is like my bones are vibrating of their own accord. Anyone else might think they were going crazy, but I choose to see it as a sign.

Something good has to happen for me, doesn't it?

It gets harder and harder for me to write in English when I hardly ever hear it anymore and I never see it except in my own journal. My Masters have allowed me to have books, but they are all written in Russian. The English words don't look spelled correctly to me on the paper even though I am pretty sure they are. Some of my favorite moments here in camp are when the miners try out their English on me after they had given me a good fuck, because it allows me to hear my native tongue again.

I've been imprisoned here at this mining camp for close to four years now. I only know that because each night that I have been here, I have scratched another mark onto the rough-hewn planks that comprise the floor and walls of my room. I have two more marks to make for the year and then I will depressingly move to another wall and start a new list.

It is hard to believe that the anniversary of my kidnapping is approaching again. I refuse to believe that this is going to be my life – that I am going to be trapped as a sex slave to a group of min-

ers who appreciate my skills but have nothing to which to compare them. I have tried to remain positive for most of my imprisonment, but as this anniversary approaches it is increasingly harder to do so. This is one of the few times that I allow myself to remember my former life and feel sorry for the loss of it.

By the age of twelve I felt like something amazing was going to happen to me in my life. When I received the bright blue mark on the side of my face at the exact moment of my thirteenth birthday, I thought maybe that was the amazing thing, but now I am not so sure. I honestly don't know how something special was ever going to happen to me in this place. My imprisonment is starting to wear on my ability to be positive.

It has been more than a year since the owner of the mine died. I hadn't cared for him since he was the man who had bought me from the kidnappers and brought me here, but he had treated me with respect and taught me to read Russian. The new owner already had a Servant when he took over, so he gave me to the miners.

It is almost the end of shift now . . .

"What's your name?"

I looked up at the big oaf who was on top of me asking the question. He was new to the mine or at least to be allowed to visit me. His face was smudged with soot and he smelled like cabbage. At least he was young and had a decent body, which was more than I could say for most of the miners here.

"They call me Drotik," I said evenly. I thought back to the last time that anyone had said my real name. It had been the day I was taken from my home in South Carolina. My captors had never spoken to me and certainly never had an opportunity to use my name. I hardly remembered how my name sounded on anyone else's tongue now.

"You have a nice fucking hole, Drotik," the big man said.

He had me bent in half with my ankles on his shoulders. His fat cock was spreading my anal ring open wide even after he had busted his nut deep inside me.

This guy wasn't the best fuck I had ever had, but he could get better. Most of the men who came to see me multiple times would let me direct them so that they could get even more out of the experience. Some of the men just wanted to bang me, call me names when they finished, which I guessed helped them to feel better about themselves, and leave as fast as they could.

In my heart, I knew that I wanted to meet and have a relationship with someone. At this point in my life, I knew that I wanted, no, *needed*, a man that was confident, self-assured, and a dominant. I had met a lot of men and nothing turned me on like a man who controlled me but respected me at the same exact time. That was the man for me.

"Thank you," I said back mechanically. "Your cock is as impressive as an ox and you fuck with the grace of a Bolshoi dancer." I had been given this line to say by the former owner of the mine. He had requested that I say it to him after each fuck. I now said it to each of the miners after they busted a nut inside my still-tight ass.

The new miner reached up and ran a dirty thumb over the brilliant blue mark on my face. He bore down like he was seeing if it would come off as he rubbed it.

He asked, "How did you get here, Drotik?"

This was not the first time that one of the miners had asked me this question. I had a standard short response to give them, but something felt different today. "I was taken from my home about a year after my mark appeared. It was my fault because I followed a handsome man into an alley to blow him and instead got a hood thrown over my head. The next thing I knew, I was in a cargo hold of a ship headed here."

"And you've been here ever since?"

"Yes."

"Have you ever been able to contact your family?"

"No. Why? Do you know a way that I could accomplish that?" I asked hopefully.

He shook his head. "I'm sorry that has happened to you, but at the same time, it is so exciting to be able to fuck you after a long day of mining."

This wasn't a terrible place to be. It wasn't my choice of course, but the men were mostly nice to me and some were even respectful. Some of them even brought me extra food or chocolate. I had a whole windowsill of carved wooden figures that some of the men had made for me. Too bad the windowsill was nailed shut.

I had tried to run away multiple times, only to be captured and beaten for my efforts. The fire of escape still burned in my heart every day that I was kept here, but I was more tempered and patient now. I would not try again without a solid viable plan.

"What's your name?" I asked as the miner rolled off of me and lit a cigarette.

"Petor," he said after taking a drag off of the hand-rolled cigarette.

"How long have you been working at the mine, Petor?" My Russian was much improved over four years. It had truly been torture when I couldn't communicate with anyone. Thanks to the tutoring of the former owner and my voracious appetite for reading, I was able to learn the native language pretty quickly.

"I came three weeks ago. It took me that long to get into the bucket."

Other men who had visited me told me how the system worked. Each man that mined his quota got his name added to the bucket each day. At the end of each day, two names were drawn—the dirty and the clean. The first one was the dirty because the man got to come straight from the mine to my room. The second name was the clean, because he came to me after dinner once he had been given the chance to take a shower. Each day that you made your quota, you increased your chance of winning.

"You mean you only met your quota once?" I asked in disbelief.

"Yeah," he admitted.

"Lucky bastard," I said with a laugh. His name was only in the bucket once, yet it was still pulled. "I bet the men were furious that your name got picked."

"They were fucking livid," he said, starting to laugh.

"I've heard some men's names are in there twelve or thirteen times just waiting."

"Vladmir told me that his is in there twenty times," Petor said with a sly smile.

"No way," I said. These little talks that I had with each of the miners every day were my salvation from going insane. They kept me informed of what was going on in and around the camp, which was vital to my plans of escape. It also gave me some semblance of normalcy in my abnormal predicament.

"Can we fuck again?" the miner asked as he put his cigarette out on the wall.

"I can," I said with a raised eyebrow.

"I definitely can," Petor said. "God only knows when I will get another chance."

I rolled over and lifted myself onto all fours. I enjoyed sex more than most normal people, I believed. Even though most of these men were not physically attractive to me, I did enjoy the sex most of the time. The men seemed to really enjoy my ass as well. Often I wondered if it made me a bad person to enjoy being fucked by men who were keeping me as their sex slave.

"You better make it count then, Petor."

Later, I showered in cold water as usual. I came out of the bathroom drying off and saw that my dinner had been delivered. It reminded me that even though this was my room, it didn't belong to me and I was not safe here.

One naked light bulb hung from the ceiling. It completely lit my room in very harsh light. My room had the only private shower in the camp besides the big house where the owner lived with his Servant. I also had the only queen bed in the camp. The owner had a king and all the miners slept in bunks.

It was a warm day, so I sat naked on the bed and ate my dinner. It gave me plenty of time to think of a way to escape. I certainly wasn't going to spend much time thinking about the stew. It was as lacking in flavor as most of the food they served here. Each day I was thankful for the tins of salt and pepper that one man had brought with him and presented to me.

Putting my dirty dishes on the tray and setting it by the door, I got myself ready for the clean miner. A chill ran up my spine just as the darkening night surprisingly lit up with numerous bright bursts of blue light. I stepped to the window and tried to see what was happening.

The night was quiet—too quiet. I couldn't hear anything and the bright sharp lights that I had seen had stopped. My bones seemed to vibrate again. Something was happening.

Suddenly a brilliant flash of light illuminated my door and before I could even think about moving, my door burst open and a cloud of smoke rolled inside. A giant hooded figure in black stepped through the door. He walked right up to me, placed his hand on my forehead, and a voice appeared inside my head.

My natural response was to pull away from the man's hand, but something told me not to. His touch had a calming effect on the weird symphony that my bones were playing. I am not a small man, myself. I stood taller than six foot three and had the body of an American football player. Very few men intimidated me physically, but this stranger did just that.

We are not here to hurt you. Come with us and we will see you safely out of this place.

It was super-unnerving to have someone inside my head, but what he was saying to me was exactly what I wanted to hear. I could tell that he was speaking a foreign language in my thoughts, but I had absolutely no problems translating the words into English even though I only spoke two languages — English and broken Russian. These thoughts, as far as I could tell, were neither.

"Who are you?" I asked out loud. I still had not seen the hooded figure's face, but I somehow could feel that he was trustworthy.

The stranger stepped back from me. He was a huge figure of a man dressed in all black. His duster jacket concealed a very large body. Upon closer inspection, I saw that he was wearing a mask of some sort. It was of a plain man's face, but it was painted jet black.

When he spoke, it was in English. "We are your rescuers. Now, come with us quickly, and we will answer all of your questions once we are safe." He held out his hand to me.

"Where will we go?"

"To safety."

"Okay," I finally relented. "I'll get dressed."

"No need," he said, as he reached down and pulled a piece of grass that was growing up through the floorboards of my room. The cloaked figure held it between his palms and dipped his head over it. One hand went up and out toward me, I saw a flash of light, and felt a heaviness settle upon me.

Looking down, I saw that I was fully dressed, in clothes that I had never seen before. I was suddenly dressed in jeans, work boots, a tank top, and a worn flannel shirt. I could feel socks on my feet and underwear under my jeans.

"Whoa." I exhaled and immediately looked up at the hooded figure in front of me. I grabbed my journal off of the table and moved forward, taking his hand. If this man could do that, then I didn't want to be on his bad side. His hand was over-sized and rough like he was a man who was used to manual labor. I was close enough to him now that I thought I could smell him. He smelled like freshly mown hay, which I was highly allergic to.

"Good choice," he said, as he turned and pulled me after him out the door.

My nose wrinkled up. His smell was starting to have an effect on me. I swallowed to try to clear my throat.

It was dark outside now, but there was enough light coming from the doorway for me to see a huge motorcycle parked in the mud in front of my cabin. Everything on the motorcycle was painted black. I looked down the street and saw nothing, but now I could hear the sounds of at least two other motorcycles in the camp.

"Get on. I'll put your book in the saddlebag."

I straddled the seat of the cycle as I watched him reach down and pick up a rock. He pointed his hand to the sky and bowed his head. Fireworks—green in color—shot from his raised hand into the sky.

At this point, it didn't seem strange to me that I was being rescued by a wizard on a motorcycle. I was still so shocked with his trick of making clothing appear out of thin air that nothing else he could do was as amazing.

I sneezed abruptly.

The wizard's fireworks must have signaled his friends.

Noise erupted in my ears as two more motorcycles joined us driven by the same hooded figures like the one that was climbing on the bike in front of me. One cycle pulled up on each side of us and the hooded masked men driving them nodded to me.

"Wrap your arms around my stomach or hold onto my shoulders," the wizard ordered, loudly enough to be heard over the engines.

I sneezed again.

I put both of my hands around the big man's waist and held on as all three motorcycles pulled away from the cabin. Within a minute, we were out of the mining camp and onto the open road. I didn't know where we were headed or who I was with, but I had never felt more alive.

I sneezed and my nose started to run. My throat was an itchy mess and my eyes even itched.

We slowed down for a fork in the road and came to a stop. The big man to our left reached over and took the hand of my wizard. I watched in awe as the man to our right reached out and pulled a leaf from a tree hanging over the side of the road before doing the same thing. All three heads bowed and there was a flash of sharp blue light.

I sneezed and tried to blow my nose on the sleeve of the magical flannel shirt that I was wearing.

The men disconnected and we pulled down one fork of the dark road. Immediately, I saw what magic my rescuers had made—there was little wind and very little road noise. It was like they had put up an invisible windshield right in front of all three motorcycles.

When the wizard in front of me spoke again, he didn't even have to raise his voice. "Hold on, marked one. You are having a reaction to something so I'm going to put you into a trance. But, I have to make sure that you don't fall off, either."

Put me into a trance?

Suddenly my head started to get foggy, and I blinked to try to focus my eyes on the road. Locking my arms around the huge man in front of me, I lay my head down on his back and closed my eyes. I didn't feel like sneezing anymore, just sleeping.

It was the last thing I remembered.

CHAPTER TWO

Part of a ledger page from the Trad Grimoire written by the Coven Master after the night of the rescue.

April second, two thousand and nineteen

Our operations into southeastern Russia went very well tonight. Our main focus was securing four marked men from a munitions base near Norilsk. We were able to secure all four of them without harm coming to anyone or without having a major problem. Hopefully, my men were able to get in and out without drawing too much attention. The last thing we need is a major international incident.

Our secondary mission tonight was to rescue a solitary marked man from a mining camp near the munitions base. We had heard reports of him for a couple of years now, but had not until recently been able to locate him. When I saw on the map that the mine was within ten kilometers of the military base, I knew that I wanted to try to perform the double rescue. I put Sloven in charge of the secondary target and he took two of his best men with him. The marked man was safely obtained and once again, the mission went off without loss of life or property.

The five marked men will rest today, and tonight I will speak with them concerning their options. If they decide to join us, we will have new members and welcome them in. If they decide to return home, we will work out the details of their journeys.

I have to attend to a small matter in Bulgaria that is causing us some headaches, but I should be back in plenty of time to speak with these new men when they are ready. There is something strange going on with me physically that I will have to consult the

elders about. It is a strange vibration from inside me — more antic-
ipatory excitement than alarm . . .

I woke with a start, still on the back of the vibrating motorcycle. I had a clear head and my memory seemed to be in-
tact. Reaching up and touching my head, I was surprised to
find that it didn't hurt. I had been drugged several times at
the mining camp where I was held prisoner for the last four
years and always woke up with a splitting headache.

A sneeze tore through my sinus cavity and brought me
out of my head.

"Are you awake, marked man?" the wizard in front of me
asked with a tone of disbelief.

"Yes," I answered.

"We just crossed the border and we will be home shortly," he informed me.

Within ten minutes, we were pulling off of the road onto a
dirt one that seemed to go for miles. There were multiple
roads that veered off in different directions. The wizards
seemed to know exactly which road to take. Soon, we pulled
into a clearing and I saw a cabin in the trees.

The big man stopped the bike and put down the kick-
stand. I promptly sneezed again. He stood, extracted himself
from the motorcycle, and turned to face me.

"Get off the bike, marked man," he commanded me with
his deep voice.

It must be morning, because the cloudy dark-purple sky
was beginning to lighten quickly. "Where are we?" I raised
my leg over the seat of the motorcycle and gingerly stood on
the rocky ground. This place was in the woods, which had
been cleared to resemble some type of huge campsite.

"Romania," he answered. I saw that the big man who had
saved me had removed his hood and taken off his mask, and
I saw what he looked like for the first time. He was super-

handsome, even in this low light. He was blond with a military buzz cut with an inch or so of longer hair protruding out above his forehead. Muscles with dark tattoos formed sleeves on each huge arm. I practically drooled at the size of his biceps and pecs.

"Romania?" I asked in wonder. Of all of the answers that I might have guessed to that question, Romania was not one of them.

"Yes. This is our camp. You are safe here. Go to that cabin there," he said pointing, "and wash the road off of you. I will bring you something to eat and show you to a place where you can sleep."

"Who are you?" I asked.

"My name is Sloven. Now, go," he commanded.

"Yes, sir." I wanted to ask him more questions, but something told me that he was not going to answer any more for me at the moment. I walked toward the cabin Sloven had indicated and slowly pushed the door open.

This cabin was nothing like the one in which I had been held for the last few years. This cabin was well-made by an expert craftsman. I could tell just from the door, which was beautifully carved with intricate pictures of nature scenes. The door to the cabin had a hammered bronze porch light that looked beautifully handmade.

"Hello?" I called from the doorway.

There was nothing but silence in return. I took a whiff and recognized the smell of Pine-Sol. This cabin had recently been scrubbed clean.

I stepped inside and closed the door. The inside of the cabin was brightly illuminated with lamps and recessed lighting. Fine rugs covered the floor, painted nature scenes hung on the walls, and comfortable couches and leather chairs dotted the living room. The furniture looked expensive. I noticed the kitchen, but moved into the bedroom instead.

The air in the cabin was cool like it was air conditioned, but I didn't see any vents or units anywhere. The windows all appeared to be closed and locked behind crisp curtains.

A huge bed with a wooden frame dominated the room. The comforter looked soft and new. It didn't escape my notice that there were two bottles of lube on the nightstand. The bathroom was off of the bedroom, so I went inside and started to wipe myself with a wet washcloth. I was surprised that I wasn't grimier than I turned out to be. Maybe that magical windshield had helped to keep me clean, even in my trance state.

I used the bathroom and made the most of the mirror time that I had. Noticing how different I looked from four years ago, I marveled at how thin I had become. Finally, I exhaled a big breath and made my way back to the living room. I was excited to have the possibility of getting to go home soon, and I couldn't wait to see if that was going to happen.

Sloven was waiting for me on the couch when I emerged from the bedroom. He stood up when I walked over toward him. "Better?" he asked.

I wrinkled my nose at his smell. "Better. How did you know to speak English to me back at the mine, Sloven?"

"I was in your head, remember?" Sloven's face held no hint of whatever emotion he was feeling.

"How did you do that?" I asked right before sneezing very hard.

"It will all be explained in due time," Sloven told me. "Is it me that you are reacting so dramatically to?"

"I think so," I admitted. "You smell like hay which I am really allergic to."

"Hay?" he asked with a stunned look on his face. "You think I have a smell?"

"It's like you rolled around in it," I admitted with a face that told him that I was sorry.

"I can fix that," he said evenly. He pulled something green out of his cargo shorts and bowed his head over it. His smell immediately changed to one of fresh mint.

"How nice," I said. "I'm not allergic to mint."

The big man looked at me like I had just pulled a knife on him. He finally cocked his head and said, "Good. Would you like to go get something to eat before you sleep?"

"Sure." I was still pretty wound up from the last few hours and from the knowledge that I was no longer a prisoner. Well, at least I hoped that I was no longer a captive. "I thought you were going to bring me something to eat."

"I was but then I found out that our primary mission tonight had just arrived, and I thought you might want to meet some of the others that we rescued."

"Others?" It had never occurred to me that there might be others beside myself that were in my same predicament. I'm pretty sure that if there had been another marked man held captive in the mining camp, I would have known about it.

"Yes, there are others."

"I would like to meet them," I said decisively.

"Follow me," Sloven ordered.

I followed the big man out of the cabin and toward what seemed to be a central building built in the round. "This is our meeting hall," Sloven explained to me as he held the door open for me.

Inside the meeting hall were round tables with six chairs at each. I looked over to see that four marked men were seated at one of the tables. They looked Eastern European and they looked up at me in unison with wide eyes. The smell of eggs, sausage, and coffee threatened to make me lightheaded.

"They were just rescued last night like you," Sloven informed me.

"Do they speak English?"

"Russian," he said with a sly smile.

I rushed over to their table and greeted the men. The looks on their faces immediately relaxed as they saw my mark and heard my Russian.

"They saved you, too?" one of the men named Teo asked me.

"Yes, just tonight," I told them as I sat down at the table. Sloven brought two plates of food over to us while another very handsome man who smelled like fresh ginger brought three more.

"Well, hello, ginger," I said with a smirk.

The man who smelled like ginger stopped in his tracks. He looked at Sloven and something passed between them. "You smell me?" he asked after staring at me for a couple of seconds.

"Yeah. It's a good smell, unlike some people," I said, making a dig at Sloven.

"Eat, Drotik," Sloven ordered.

It turned out that the men had been held at a military facility not too far from the mine where I had been held. I only knew that because they told me. I had no clue of my surroundings, but apparently they had more information.

"What is this place?" the one called Tomcjk asked.

"I'm not sure, but they are a lot nicer than the people at the mine," I answered. "Did that big dark-haired guy rescue you?"

"Yes," one of them answered. "His name is Thom."

"Is the other one the one who rescued you?"

I nodded. "Sloven."

A short man named Sqo asked, "Have you seen him do anything strange?"

"You mean the magic?"

All of them shook their heads and looked at me in wonder. We were quiet for a minute while we ate. Our rescuers soon were at the table with five cups of coffee.

"Can I have cream and sugar, Sloven?" I asked almost flirtatiously.

"American," he mumbled under his breath.

I was used to drinking my coffee the Russian way—very black and very strong, but the idea of having a cup of coffee the way I wanted it was too alluring to me. Secretly, I also enjoyed making Sloven jump through some hoops for me.

Sloven left to get me the items I had asked for.

"I wonder why they just don't make it appear," I said.

"I wonder what they want with us," Sqo said.

"What all NOMARs want," I said.

NOMARs, or non-marked men, were the vast majority of the men in our world. They were sexually attracted to women, which our world did not contain, so they were constantly horny and sexually frustrated.

Marked men were sexually attracted to other men, so on one hand they had a whole world of men to choose to fuck around with, but on the other their very nature opened themselves up to abuse. There was nothing a NOMAR would like better than owning a sex slave.

If I had not been kidnapped in the United States and brought to Russia, I would have entered a special school for marked men called The Service Academy where I would have spent several years learning how to sexually please a man. Then I could have entered The Service and sold myself to a wealthy NOMAR.

I was more than willing to be a sex slave for pay on my own terms. The Service would have produced a contract between me and the wealthy man who wanted to be my Master to pay me and keep me safe from abuse while I was indentured. These agreements usually lasted for two years, but could be extended for several more beyond that.

Each marked man that went into Service received a million dollars a year. That money would have been life-saving for my family, and I grieved for the loss of it almost as much as I did for the loss of my last four years. I was still only eighteen years of age, so maybe when I got back to the United States, I could still enter into The Service.

"These NOMARs can suck my dick," Tomcjk spat. "I'm tired of servicing men and getting nothing in return for it."

"You got a hell of a lot of fat cock up your arse for it," Sqo said with a smile.

"Well, yeah, but I wanna be paid," Tomcjk said, right as Sloven delivered my sugar and cream.

I stirred the additives into my coffee. "I dunno," I said, looking across the circular meeting hall at the two drop-dead gorgeous men. "These men are pretty fucking hot."

"Yeah, they are," Teo agreed as he drank some coffee and followed my eyes.

"You're more my type, Drotik," my new friend Sqo said, looking at me with a lusty grin on his face.

"I'm flattered, Sqo, but a bed for sleeping is all I am thinking about right now," I said with an exaggerated yawn. The coffee was having no effect on keeping me awake, but it sure tasted like heaven. "I've been up all night and not in my usual way," I said with a wink.

My four new friends laughed as I stood up with my dirty dishes. Sloven was beside me in a flash and a cloud of a minty smell. "You ready to sleep, Drotik?"

"Unless you want to fool around, Sloven," I suggested.

"The Master forbids it until you have made your decision," he said with the authority of a leader.

The Master?

"What decision?" I asked, trying to dig for information.

"The decision that you will make to the question the Master will ask you," he said infuriatingly.

"I'm ready to sleep and get some answers, but I see that I'm only going to get one of those from you."

"Now, you're getting smart . . ."

"Will we see each other again?" I asked the big man as I pointed at my new friends.

"Yes. You will see them tonight when you all will make an appearance in front of the Master."

I translated that into Russian for my tablemates and then waved goodbye to them. Sloven led me toward the door and then back into the cabin where I had washed earlier.

"Is this your cabin, Sloven?" I asked.

"No."

I looked at him in disgust. "You're not going to tell me anything, are you?"

He smiled and said, "Not if I can help it. You can sleep peacefully. I will be right here if you need anything."

"Aren't you tired?" I asked him in shock. "You were up all night and drove home."

"I took a tonic, so I will be good to stand guard over you while you sleep," he promised me.

"Do I have to be protected? Am I in danger?"

"Everything needs to be protected," he said mysteriously.

"Some things more than others," I told him as I turned and let him get a good look of my ass in these magical jeans. I headed to the bedroom without turning around, but I could still hear him snort.

I was still chuckling to myself as I stripped off my clothes and climbed under the covers. I was exhausted, but at least my spirit was making a comeback.

CHAPTER THREE

Part of a journal entry from the Russian sex slave known as Drotik written on the second of April, two thousand nineteen.

I am so thankful that I was allowed to grab my journal before leaving the mining camp. It helps me think to be able to write about the things that happen to me each day.

I'm very intrigued about what is happening at this camp where I have been brought. I have met only the two wizards so far, but I know there are more. There seems to be a whole side of the camp that we have not been able to see yet.

I really enjoy being around the other marked men here. I have never been around others of my kind. There were no marked men in my hometown growing up and I was taken before I was old enough to go to The Service Academy, so this is the first time that I have ever even been able to talk to a marked man.

I have discovered that my four Russian friends are coupled up, which surprised me at first because I have such a thing for NOMARs that I never even considered having sex with another marked man. Sqo told me that marked men frequently fall in love with each other, but I know in my heart that it would take a big burly man like Sloven to satisfy me. Does that make me less of a man to admit or a traitor to my mark? I'm not sure, but I definitely know what turns me on and I will always follow my cock.

Something is supposed to happen tonight according to Sloven. That's all he would tell me. He has said from the start that the Master would speak to us and ask for our decision on something, so maybe that is who we are waiting on. I have a lot of questions that I will ask this Master when he appears, like when am I going home and how am I getting there?

Later that day, after I had slept, I ate again and spent quite a lot of time talking to the other marked guys that had been saved last night like me. It was obvious that we were waiting for something to happen, but no one seemed to want to tell us what that was.

My four Russian friends were older than me, probably in their twenties, but each of them looked much older than that. The two wizards who were serving as our hosts were probably in their late thirties, if I was judging. I had a real thing for older men, so I was digging both of them. I was also horny as hell, so I made a mental note to try to get Sloven into my bed tonight.

As soon as dinner was over, Sloven and Thom escorted us to a clearing in the woods. There was a round fire pit in the middle and the larger circle around it had been swept clean of almost everything except pine needles.

Sloven addressed us in English, saying, "Marked men, tonight you get an opportunity that could possibly change the rest of your lives. Tonight, you will meet the Master and he will offer you a huge opportunity. You are free to listen and make your decision. If at that time you decide to not take the opportunity, you will be given transport home."

Sloven paused dramatically while we stared at him intently and gave me a chance to repeat his words in Russian for my friends.

He continued, "Would you like to stay to meet the Master?"

Again, I translated.

"Yes," we answered in unison.

"Excellent," he said. "Please strip and put your clothes here," he told us as he indicated a stump outside of the circle. "Do not step into the circle until we have given you permission."

I watched as Thom picked up a twig off of the circle floor. He held it between his palms and bowed his head. Opening his hands, he held his palms out over the logs in the fire pit and immediately orange flames blazed around them.

The Russian boys were already stripping, so I started to remove my clothing as well. "Do you think we are going to get fucked by them?" I asked.

"God, I hope so."

"Can you imagine what magic they could do while fucking?" Sqo asked before all of us started to giggle.

"Silence!" Sloven called to us.

I looked up to see him using a long branch to scratch a pentagram into the circle with the blazing fire as the middle. Hooking my thumbs into the elastic of my underwear, my bones started to vibrate again. It was a weird feeling that I thought had passed, but now it was back with a vengeance — more intense than before.

Teo asked, "What's wrong, Drotik?"

"Nothing," I lied. "Just a chill," I explained as I shook myself like I was having a cold chill.

"I could warm up that big cock of yours," the Russian named Provan told me with a wink.

"Yeah, that's a big prick you got, Drotik," Sqo said. "We could have fun with that."

I laughed at the faces my Russian friends were making until I saw Sloven approaching us.

He looked at us to make sure we were completely naked and said, "It is time."

We followed him to the circle. He pointed at one leg of the star etched into the dirt and said, "Sqo."

We moved to the next leg where he put Teo and the next one where Provan was placed. Tomcjk was next and then I was kneeling at the fifth and final point of the pentagram.

The weird vibration of my bones had continued to ratchet up until I felt like I was visibly shaking as I knelt. But then, movement in the trees took my focus away from what my body was doing.

At first, I thought it was the one they were calling the Master, but then I saw that it was a large group of people. Movement to the side drew my attention where I saw Thom and Sloven removing their shirts. They both had amazing chests that were covered with fur.

Looking back at the group of men coming through the trees, I now saw that they also had their shirts off. Each of these men was built like a brick shithouse, one more stunningly handsome than the next. My eyes were full of the sight of more than twenty big men coming my way.

I was still ogling the half-naked men when I saw the group that was behind them. Eight smaller men were in line behind the wizards. They were naked except for thin red robes that they were wearing. The sides of the robes did not meet in the front, so they were fully exposed from the front. The most remarkable thing about those men was the brilliant blue marks on the sides of their faces.

The light from the fire caused the blue marks on the men's faces to seem to jump around. I had thought that our group of five marked men together was a big deal, but here was a group of eight. My whole body tingled at the thought of what those eight men do for the wizards.

The wizards aligned themselves around two thirds of the arc of the circle. The marked men in red robes stood on the remaining third of the circle directly across from me.

My bones were still vibrating, but now my cock instantly got hard. Something was about to happen.

"Bow your heads, marked men," Sloven announced loudly.

I bowed my head. I didn't really need to see because my body was telling me everything I needed to know at this point. I had figured out that whatever was going on with me was related to the Master coming.

My bones were positively vibrating out of my limbs and my cock was harder than I ever remembered it being before, until suddenly my whole body except my prick went quiet.

He was here . . .

I didn't know about anyone else, but for me it was like the oxygen had been sucked out of the clearing. I couldn't hear a bird, squirrel, or insect in the woods for the first time, as if all life forms showed this man respect.

"He's wearing a talisman," a deep sexy voice called out to the assemblage. I couldn't be sure, but it sounded like the wizards were speaking in that language that sounded foreign but that I could easily understand.

What the fuck is a talisman?

"Who Master?" I recognized Sloven's voice.

"The big one," the deep voice of the Master called.

Oh, shit. I was pretty sure that he was talking about me. I was much bigger than all the other marked men.

"He's completely naked, Master," Sloven said, stating the obvious.

"I am drawn to him, Sloven. Like no man that I have ever experienced before. He has to have an object on him that is drawing my force to him. Search him," the Master commanded.

He's drawn to me? What does that mean?

I heard a rustling amongst the gathered men and then some whispers. "Silence!" Sloven said angrily. "Thom, grab those two branches there," Sloven called across the circle.

"Stand, Drotik," Sloven ordered.

I stood and looked up. The Master was not in my eye sight. He must have been behind me.

As soon as I stood up, the assembled men all got a good

look at my rock-hard cock, but not a sound was made about it. I watched in fascination as Thom approached me carrying two sticks. Sloven met him with a third. They put the branches together and formed a triangle.

The two big men knelt with the triangle of branches and laid it on the ground at my feet.

"Do you have anything on you?" Sloven asked me. His blue eyes implored me to not make a fuss.

"No, sir."

"Do you have anything inside of you?" he asked.

"Inside of me?" I asked in shock.

"Answer his fucking question," the Master said from right behind me. His deep sexy voice made the hairs on the back of my neck stand at attention.

"No, sir."

"Step into the triangle and hold still," Sloven ordered.

I stepped over one of the branches and held myself steady inside the triangle formed by them. Sloven and Thom reached down, grabbed the branches, bowed their heads, and slowly lifted the branches up.

Watching the triangle rise around me, I realized that I was holding my breath. I blew it out just as the branches rose toward my neck and then over my head.

"He's clean, Master," Sloven finally said as he took the branches and threw them out of the circle.

"How is that possible?" the deep voice called from behind me.

No one answered him.

I was keenly aware that I was still standing when suddenly he appeared in front of me. I felt my mouth drop open and my head tilt back.

The Master was at least six foot five. Rarely did I have to look up to anyone, but this man was an exception. He had long jet-black hair that was shiny and pulled back into a ponytail that hung over the hair from the back of his head that swept his shoulders. He had a full black beard and mustache that framed a very handsome face. Dark eyes penetrated my very being from his beautiful face.

"What's your name, marked man?" he demanded.

I swallowed hard and said, "Drotik, sir."

"Drotik, *Master*," he corrected me immediately.

I nodded.

"Say it," he growled.

"Drotik, Master," I said as my heart started to pound out of my chest. The smell of honeysuckle filled my nostrils. It was one of my favorite smells from childhood, so I breathed in deeply of it, realizing that there was a masculine musk behind it as well.

"That name is bullshit," he spat. "We don't honor Russian here."

I was struck speechless. The Master had his shirt off and I couldn't help but look down and then stare at his body. He was probably in his late forties, but you would never be able to tell from his physique. He was fabulously built and thick as a bodybuilder. I couldn't wait for him to be on top of me where I could hold onto his thick biceps as he fucked down into me. His chest was shaved smooth and his biceps were covered in heavy black tattoos that totally turned me on.

"It is Dart in English, is it not?" he asked me.

"Yes, Master." *Smart and big . . .* It had almost been a year after they started calling me that for me to learn Russian enough to know what it meant and why they used it for me.

The ends of his lips turned up at my correct use of his title. He proclaimed, "Then you will be known as Dart here."

"Why is your cock so hard, Dart?" he asked as he reached out with a thick powerful hand and wrapped it around my painfully erect prick.

As soon as our skins touched a brilliant blue spark flashed

through the dark woods and temporarily blinded me. The Master pulled his hand away from me and when I could see again, he was staring at me with wide dark eyes.

"What are you?" he asked me in almost a whisper.

"I could ask the same of you, Master. I am equally drawn to you as you are to me and your cock is just as hard as mine," I said with a head nod to the tremendous bulge in the front of his jeans.

"You will not ask anything of me, Dart," he said deeply. "But I will figure out who the hell you are, trust me."

"I will be more than grateful to allow you to explore the whole of me in order to answer your questions, Master," I said, tongue in cheek. By now, I had figured out that he was the source of the awesome smell. I couldn't get enough of his scent.

"You will do as I command," he snapped. "Now, kneel and bow your head, Dart."

I quickly fell to my knees onto the pine needles and bowed my head. This was the most exciting man that I had ever met. I was intrigued by him and loved his command already. From my new stance, I was able to see that the Master was barefoot and his feet were amazing—big and masculine, clean and well groomed. I prayed to God that I got to suck on them soon.

When the Master spoke again, he had moved away from me. His voice was louder in order to project out to all of the assembled men. His voice was doing that strange interpretation thing again.

"Welcome, marked men. We are the Vrajitor motorcycle gang."

The assembled men all around the circle said, "Sain baculum."

The Master continued, "Look at me, honored marked men."

I looked up right into his dark gaze. The Master seemed to be completely focused on me and it sent a jolt of energy down my spine and into my hard prick.

"It was our honor to rescue you from your dire circumstances and now we offer you an opportunity. You are welcome to hear our pitch and you are free to decide what you would like to do. All we ask is that if you choose to return to your lives, that you do not speak of us again. Do you agree?"

The five of us kneeling answered, "Yes, Master."

Master said, "I will bind you to my bidding."

I looked up to see him reach down and grab a pine needle from the ground. He held it between his palms and bowed his head. A pulse of energy radiated out from him through the five of us.

"What I tell you now will probably be hard to believe, but it is the truth." He paused for dramatic effect, even though the situation didn't need it. This was the most intense thing that I had ever been a part of.

The Master continued, "We are warlocks. We are a family. Some people call it a coven or a trad, but we prefer gang."

This didn't surprise me because the name of his gang had already translated to the word *warlock* in my brain by whatever magical trick they were using. I had thought them wizards, but they were warlocks. While wizards were more akin to magicians, warlocks were grounded in nature for their magic like witches.

"Our magic is used only for good. We work with and in nature to accomplish what we believe needs to be done to better the world. I'm sure that you have seen some remarkable things since you have been with us."

The Master continued by saying, "Which brings us to the opportunity that we have for you. We very much want to fuck you."

He is direct . . .

CHAPTER FOUR

Part of a ledger page from the Trad Grimoire written by the Coven Master on the third of April, two thousand nineteen

I am disappointed to have to write that my physical symptoms still persist today. I was able to get some relief when I visited Bulgaria yesterday, but as soon as I crossed the Romanian border my bones started to vibrate even stronger than before.

Once I got to camp, I had a raging hard-on that I couldn't seem to get rid of despite fucking two of the gang Servants. I left to make a trip to see the Elders about this problem within the hour of returning home.

I met with the Elders who listened patiently while I described my symptoms. They consulted ancient Grimoires and also brewed a portent potion. They spent over an hour stirring the thick liquid until they were ready to reveal their thoughts. They explained that they were conflicted but had finally come to a consensus that they could live with.

I know that the Elders are rarely wrong, but I have to believe that this time they have it wrong. The Elders have predicted that a rival to me has or will arrive at camp. I have only been the Coven Master for two years and usually a rival does not appear for twenty.

If they are correct, then we will have to have a spell battle to see who is most deserving of being the Master. It is not something that I take lightly or look forward to. The painful memory of the former Master's death still hangs heavy over me, and I do not relish having to battle again.

I have come back to camp with a heavy heart, only to have my body resonate with the vibrations of my rival's approach again. I guess it will come to a head here either tonight or tomorrow.

I was still kneeling on the pine needles in the middle of the darkened forest. The only light was from the fire in the middle of the circle, but it was surprisingly bright. The huge coven Master was standing toward the middle of the circle. He had just told us that he was the leader of a motorcycle gang who were also warlocks. He had also just said that they wanted to fuck us. It was a lot to process in such a short time.

The Master's deep voice rang out in the clearing once more. "Our magic is grounded in nature, and sex is the most natural act there is. So, we have found over the hundreds of years that we have been practicing witchcraft that our most powerful magic is done while we are fucking. It not only brings us pleasure, but increases our spellwork substantially."

I bet it does . . .

The head warlock turned to view everyone inside and on the circle, but his gaze always returned to me, giving me the impression that he was speaking directly to me. Maybe he was or maybe he was trying to figure out why he was drawn to me so.

"Unlike that Russian scum that we rescued you from, we do not rape marked men. But you are in a position to help us. Each of the five of you has a unique skill set that we are more than willing to pay for. If you accept this opportunity, we will negotiate with each of you for a salaried position in our organization."

We have unique skills that they are willing to pay for? Makes us sound like a bunch of whores, but it is really the same thing as a contract with a wealthy NOMAR — sex for cash.

The Master let this information sink in for a full minute while he slowly walked around the outside of the fire and stared at each one of us. His dark gaze was at once unnerving and tremendously sexually exciting to me. I couldn't help but picture myself bending to his will. And by bending to his will, I was more than ready to let him bend me in half and fuck the shit out of me.

"You will be safe here with us. You will be wealthy here with us. You will be valued and pampered here with us. You may leave of your own free will at any time. If you don't believe me, please ask the marked men who serve us now. They have made far more money than from any Service contract that they could ever have negotiated. Each one of them has kneeled in your place. Each one of them was rescued by us and chose to work with us to better the world. Others have come, knelt in your place, chosen to not accept this opportunity, and then been returned home safely."

I was just wondering how my group of marked men were going to be able to speak to his group when the Master pulled a smooth river rock out of his jeans pocket and clasped it between his palms.

"My brothers and I will give you some time to talk," he said right before he pulled his hands apart and then smashed them together again. With an explosive flash, all of the warlocks disappeared.

My marked friends and I were still looking around in amazement when the red-robed marked men filtered over to us. One of them was clearly in charge and he didn't look happy.

"I am Stephan, the head Servant," he said to the five of us as we gathered into one group. "I know you speak English, but do they?" he asked me.

"They only speak Russian," I informed him.

He snarled at me, "Then you will have to translate. We

are not allowed to speak it here."

"Can't you just use that translator magic thing so that they can understand?" I asked innocently.

"What translator thing?" he asked, looking at me like I was crazy.

I'm sure that I looked just as confused as I sounded when I said, "The one that the Master was using when he first arrived."

"The Master was using Witchspeak when he first arrived," he said with disgust. "No one knows that language except them."

And me, I guess . . .

"It is obvious that you are the Master's type, Dart, but that doesn't mean shit here. I am not threatened by you, because we have a hierarchy. The Master has been enchanted by other marked men in the past, right Torsch?" Stephan asked as he turned to one of the taller men behind him.

Torsch blushed immediately in the firelight while I translated what Stephan was saying into Russian. I also took the opportunity to ask my friends if they could understand the Master when he first arrived. They told me that they could not.

I was hoping that Torsch would have told me what happened between him and the Master, but it was obvious that he was not going to, so I asked Stephan, "And what happened?"

"The Master is a very busy man and he quickly loses interest. He is also the most powerful Warlock here, so he has a . . . great need for us. He will use you for some great magic, but then he will move on," Stephan said with all of the cockiness that he could muster.

"You will be famous for whatever great magic that he does with you," Torsch said almost reverentially.

"Yes, yes, we know all about how your famous ass saved those people in the water when that barge went down in

Thailand," Stephan said with a roll of his eyes. "The point is that the Master does not play with his toys long."

Sqo interrupted his tirade by asking some of the men behind him, "You were all rescued just like us?"

All of the marked men wearing the red robes nodded their heads. I could almost read their sad stories on their expressive faces.

So, they understand Russian, they just aren't allowed to speak it . . .

Teo asked, "And you are all free here? You can leave at any time?"

They nodded again.

"And you have earned a lot of money here?" Tomcjk asked.

"A shitload," Stephan said to me in English which I translated into Russian.

"Do they treat you well?" I asked in Russian. "Do they ever humiliate you, or physically harm you, or degrade you?" I saw my Russian friends nod their approvals at my asking this.

"Never," Stephan said. "You would be very lucky to be employed here, if it is the Master's wish."

I translated for my friends.

"Will we become . . . like them if we stay?" Pravan asked. He looked scared to death and constantly looked around him like the Warlocks were going to pop out of thin air at any minute.

Stephan answered by condescendingly saying, "You cannot just be made into a Warlock. You have to be born that way. Besides, there are no marked warlocks."

I translated and Pravan asked, "Then what are you?"

"We are the Servants of the Warlock's motorcycle gang. We are the vessels that they use to make magic. We are the special ones who are shown the attention of these beautiful men."

I translated and then asked the question that had been bugging me since the beginning, "Where do they get the money from?"

There was a popping sound, then—all of the warlocks re-appeared. The Master's deep voice boomed across the clearing. "Enough!"

That is an amazing party trick! I had to admit to myself that I was just as intrigued by the offer as by the man standing in front of me. At this point, I wasn't sure if I could really separate the two. I think I would love to stay and help these men do what they claim to do, but I had been away from my father and the United States for so long. My attraction to this man seemed physical while the longing to see my family seemed emotional, and I was conflicted by the need to just pick one. I wanted it all.

"Kneel at the points of the star, marked men," the Master commanded firmly.

I knelt, still not knowing what I was going to do. Fortunately, for me, the Master started with Sqo who was kneeling beside me.

The coven Master stood over the kneeling man and said, "Marked man known as Sqo. Do you accept the employment opportunity that the Vrajitor has offered you? Will you become their Servant and serve them faithfully? Will you give of your body in return for riches?"

I couldn't help but notice that the Master spoke to Sqo in the marked man's native tongue. The gang may have not been allowed to speak Russian, but the Master could obviously do what he wanted.

Sqo looked up into the face of the big man who had so captivated my attention. "I accept."

"I accept, *Master*," the Master growled to him.

Sqo trembled in front of the big man but was able to repeat the proper phrase.

Teo was next and he accepted. Now, I felt even more pressure because my friends were going to stay. Maybe that is what the Master was counting on when he chose to have me answer last.

The coven Master moved in front of Pravan. He said the same statement and waited for a response.

"Master," Pravan started nervously. His head was bowed to avoid making eye contact. "I . . . I . . . miss my family too much and it has been years since I have seen them. I appreciate the job offer, but if it is okay with you, I'm going to decline."

"We are sorry to see you go, Pravan." I was impressed with how sympathetic and kind the Master's tone was with the Russian marked man. "Are you absolutely sure?"

Pravan nodded his head and said, "I'm sure."

The Master of the Warlocks reached down and put something I couldn't see between his palms. He held them out toward Pravan who was suddenly fully dressed. He reached into one of his pockets and pulled out a stack of cash. It was too dark for me to see if they were Rubles or not.

"Here is one thousand US dollars, Pravan. We would appreciate that you not speak of us or tell anyone about us. We will know if you do and will not be happy," the Master said menacingly.

"I will not ever speak of it," Pravan said, and from his tone, I believed him. "I will always remember my friends though," he added, looking at the other four of us kneeling at the ends of the pentagram.

The gang leader moved forward toward Pravan, and I actually thought that the big man was going to strike my friend. Instead of hitting Pravan, the Master reached up and very delicately pulled one single strand of hair off of his head and held it in his palm.

"Where would you like to be placed, Pravan?"

Pravan looked confused for a second and then answered, "I am from South Minsk. My family is hopefully still there."

"And that is where you want taken?" the Master asked.

"Yes, please."

"Very well," the Master said as he bowed his head.

"Sain baculum," the gathered crowd said.

"Safe journey," the Master said as he opened his hands and then brought them together in a handclap.

I watched in amazement as Pravan just ceased to exist in this space. I thought I would see him fade away, but instead one second he was here and the next he was gone. I prayed that Pravan had really been transported to South Minsk and not been killed.

Tomjck was the next one that the Master approached. He stood right in front of my kneeling friend and said, "Marked man known as Tomjck. Do you accept the employment opportunity that the Vrajitor has offered you? Will you become their Servant and serve them faithfully? Will you give of your body in return for riches?"

Tomjck shot me a quick glance and then accepted.

"Excellent. We are moving right along then," the Master said as his gaze laser-locked onto mine. He quickly walked over to stand right in front of me but was careful not to touch me.

My cock was still hard as a steel beam and my body was ringing with sexual energy like the bell in Notre Dame with Quasimodo yanking the chain. The fragrant smell of flowering honeysuckle enveloped me just as I caught a whiff of his sweaty crotch which was right at my eye-level.

The big man who was the leader of the warlocks repeated the same exact statements and questions to me. I found it impossible to look away from him. His smell and his closeness threatened to overwhelm me. The smell of honeysuckle and sweaty man filled my head, making me light-headed again.

"Master . . ." I began.

"You will not disappoint me, Dart," he growled in a low guttural voice. His dark eyes dared me to disobey him.

"Master," I began again. "I very much would like to stay . . ."

"But?"

I was able to break the stare we had developed enough to look at all of the faces in the circle looking at me.

"I would like to negotiate with you alone, Master," I finally blurted out. Only then was I able to look into his eyes again.

He narrowed his eyes. "Why, little one?"

I had never been called *little one* before in my life and I had to admit that I liked it instantly. "Well, if the negotiations go well, I will accept your offer and if they do not, then I will have to decline." I didn't see how I could be any more forthright with him.

I could hear a rumbling amongst all of the warlocks and their Servants. I saw the look of intrigue on the Master's face change to annoyance.

The big man in front of me said very firmly, "That is not the way we do it. You will accept now and negotiate later."

"That is the way I will have to do it, Master."

The coven Master broke our gaze and turned to address the others. "Dart and I will move to a place where we can negotiate privately and then we will return."

Sloven said, "Master, that is—"

"I know what it is," the Master snapped. "You will all wait for us to return . . . in silence," he commanded.

"Let's go, Dart," he ordered as he nodded behind me.

I turned around and the Master put his over-sized hand on the small of my back. In the darkened woods, I saw the effects of the blue flash of light as our skins touched, but this time he did not pull it away. The blue flash soon turned into a warm spot on my lower back and then into a hot throbbing that went straight to my balls.

It was so dark that I couldn't see a thing, but the Master didn't seem to have a problem knowing where everything was. I looked up at the Master to see he was smirking down at me. "This negotiation will go my way, little one."

"I think we will both be very pleased with it, Master."

The Master reached out and pulled a small piece of moss off of a tree we passed and then held it between his hands. A red light immediately illuminated the forest floor, leading right to the door of a cabin in the dark.

"I better be, Dart. I better be."

CHAPTER FIVE

Part of a missing person's report filed every April by Drotik's father for the last four years at a police station outside of Charleston, South Carolina.

Missing person—Gage McClendon
Citizenship—United States of America
Last date that his whereabouts were known—thirtieth of March, two thousand fifteen
Age at the time of disappearance—Fourteen
Last known address—Mt. Argon High School
One hundred fourteen Rodgers Road
Charleston, South Carolina
Description—Gage is a marked man, blond hair, green eyes. He is approximately six foot three inches tall and weighs around one hundred and eighty pounds. His mark is brilliant blue in color starting from his left earlobe in a flame pattern that goes all the way down to the middle of his chin.
Closest living relative—George McClendon, father
Person filing the report—George McClendon
Narrative—Gage had just finished classes at his high school on March thirtieth. Surveillance from the school shows that Gage went to his locker after his last class and then left the building and the grounds. He headed west on Forsthye Street. He stopped at a Starbucks, where he paid for a Carmel Macchiato with his credit card. Surveillance video shows that a dark-haired man in his thirties engaged the missing person for a brief minute and then left the coffee shop. The video shows that Gage left the coffee shop, briefly looked out into a section of the . . .

I had just asked for a private audience with the coven Master to negotiate my employment and he had just escorted me to a cabin in the middle of the forest. The Master was expecting a lot from me but I was more than willing to give it to him.

The big man deftly started to turn on some lights in the cabin and asked, "What shall we begin with, little one? Something for me and then something for you? Quid pro quo, so to speak?"

This man was a lot smarter than I gave him credit for . . .

"If that is the way you want to play it, Master, then I'm game for that," I said while maintaining eye contact with him.

"You are definitely the game, little one. And I always win," he told me as he closed the gap between us, picked me up, threw me over his shoulder, and carried me to the bed.

The Master threw me down on the king-sized bed and began to unbutton the front of his jeans.

"How very Neanderthal Man of you . . ."

The Master growled and said, "When you belong to me, you will not be allowed to speak to me like that."

I sat up on the bed and asked, "When I belong to you?"

He dropped his jeans to the floor and stepped out of them. He wasn't wearing any underwear. "Yes. You will be mine, Dart."

I didn't want to get my hopes up at what he said—even though they were everything I wanted to hear him say. I had been disappointed too many times in the past to let that happen. And Stephan's words of the Master tiring of me were still echoing in my head.

My eyes were full of the sight of his gigantic cock. It might have been the biggest dick that I had ever seen, but it was also one of the most beautiful. His cock was thick and long with bulging veins that ran up and down the glorious shaft. The cock head was a big pink cap that looked like it was a stopper in a genie's bottle. I certainly hoped that something fantastic was going to be released.

The Master reached down and grabbed his junk and lifted it up and out for me to see all of it. "It's the kind of cock that ruins little boys' asses like yours," he said proudly.

"It is magnificent, Master, but I hardly think it is going to ruin me. It might make me hurt for a while, but I will be able to recover," I said confidently.

He laughed easily and said, "If I had a dollar for every man who has said the same thing."

"We will see how the negotiations go, but I will probably prove it to you," I said with a smirk.

"Your opening salvo, Dart?"

"If I may, Master?" I asked as I slid off the bed onto the thick rug in front of him.

"By all means," he said, spreading his legs and releasing his cock and balls back to their natural state, which was apparently *hard and full of cum.*

I knelt in front of the big man whom I was drawn to and grasped the root of his prick in my hand. The blue spark popped in front of my eyes and I felt the Master jerk back slightly. I held my hand there until the heat developed and threatened to overwhelm me. His sweet and manly smell enveloped me.

I leaned back slightly and looked up his muscular chest to his face. "Do you think it is going to do that when I put it in my mouth?"

"There's only one way to find out." The Master growled as he grabbed the back of my head and pulled me forward onto his prick.

There was definitely an explosion inside my mouth when I sucked the big man for the first time. While the electric spark of our skin touching was definitely there, the heat formed between my lips and his dick was unlike anything that I had ever experienced. And I had sucked a lot of cocks.

The taste of the Master's skin was beyond anything that I had expected, like a piece of fresh ginger — slightly sweet but with a bite of heat. I sucked on the large cockhead until he produced a drop of golden pre-cum, which I immediately flicked off of his piss slit with the end of my tongue.

"Fuck! You are driving me crazy." The Master groaned above me. "I want to shoot a load of my hot spunk down your throat so badly."

I took my mouth off of his big unit, massaged him with my hand, and looked up at him. "And I want to see my father in the United States," I countered.

"Oh, so this is how the negotiation is going to go?" His normally deep voice was super husky with need.

"Yes, Master," I answered as I pressed my thumb against the large bottom vein of his stiff shaft.

"If this is what a blow job costs me, what the fuck am I going to have to give you to fuck your ass?"

"I can't reveal my hand just yet, Master." I moved back over him and engulfed him inside my hot mouth. I tried my best to swallow his entire monster but could only make it three-quarters of the way down before I was starting to gag.

I could feel that he was close to the edge, despite my inability to give him the proper blowjob that I wanted to give him. The coven Master held the back of my head, stopping my forward momentum.

"Fuuuccccckkkkkk!" He growled as he pulled his hips back and then dumped a tremendous load of sperm into my mouth. As soon as I swallowed, he pushed his big cock into the back of my throat and continued to pump hot man-seed into me.

I sucked for all I was worth, trying hard to milk more of his delicious jizz out of his fuck-stick. I was still licking up and down the outside of his shaft when I felt it happen.

It felt like my heart stopped and then all the muscles in my body popped with energy. I removed my mouth from his cock and looked down at my body. It was not dramatic, but I suddenly looked like I had just worked out for the last two hours. All of my muscles were ripped and defined, almost like they had been puffed up with air.

I looked up at the Master to see if he had noticed. He was looking down at me with the strangest look on his face. I couldn't tell whether it was a look of concern, or horror, or surprise, but he was definitely confused by something.

"Are you a seeker?" he asked me suddenly.

"I don't know what—" I started to answer him when he reached down, grabbed me by the neck, and lifted me to my feet.

"A seeker. A warlock in training," he explained.

I couldn't talk with him holding my neck, so I just shook my head.

He let go of my neck and said, "You can't be a crafter, so what the fuck are you?"

"You saw what happened when my belly was full of your seed, Master?"

The Master pushed me onto the bed and crawled on top of me. He looked down at me with those dark eyes and said, "You think my cum did that to you?"

His face was so close to mine and his naked body was just inches above me. I felt hot and uncomfortable. "I think so, Master. I know that you think that I am doing something, but I really am not."

"Why do you think that it is me?"

"I had a strange reaction when I first encountered Sloven, Master and it didn't stop until . . ."

"Until I arrived," he said evenly.

"Yes, Master." I blushed.

He closed his eyes for a second and then reopened them. "Was the reaction a vibration in your—"

"Bones, Master," I finished for him. "Yes."

He looked at me in disbelief. "We need to fuck now, little one."

"But—"

"Now!" he growled. "I will give you whatever you want, Dart, but we need to fuck right now." He must have seen the look of suspicion on my face, because he added, "I will bind myself to you, if you demand it."

"Just your honor, Master," I said.

"You will let me fuck you without any binding spell?" he asked in surprise.

"If you give me your word on your honor first, Master."

"Why would you risk that, little one? I could completely screw you over afterward."

"I probably am a fool, Master, but I have a feeling about you and from what you have said, you are drawn to me also. I don't think you will be able to screw me over."

"I'm going to screw you over right now." He growled as he lifted a muscled arm and rolled me onto my stomach.

"Your word, Master," I demanded.

He huskily promised, "My word, Dart. I will give you whatever you want. My word is just as set in stone as a binding spell."

"Fuck away, Master," I said happily. I was terribly concerned that he was going to fuck me and then lose interest, but I dismissed that thought from my mind immediately, or tried to.

"This is going to be hard and fast, Dart. I'm going to drop a big load of my jizz deep inside your guts and then we are going to see what happens," the big man told me as he lifted me onto all fours on the bed.

I marveled at my new biceps as I held myself up on the

bed. "I'm going to need a lot of lube," I informed him. "You've got the biggest cock I've ever seen."

"Now you are just trying to flatter me," the Master growled from behind me as he stepped into the saddle. "No marked man in this camp has ever been able to take me on the first try and believe me when I say that they have tried their damnest."

Oh, fuck! He isn't going to use any lube? This is going to hurt like hell. I braced myself for the pain.

The Master and I were constantly touching, so small sparks of blue energy were popping constantly in the air, but in the middle of that, I saw a purple flash from behind me and instantly felt coolness on my asshole. I guessed that he was casting a spell to create lube.

"Ready, little one?"

"Ready, Master," I consented.

The coven Master grabbed both of my hips and pulled them back roughly at the same time that he pushed his hips forward. His magnificently large cock head pushed through my anal ring like an ultra-sharp arrow shot out of a crossbow.

The pain was like nothing I had ever experienced before and tears came to my clenched-shut eyes immediately. My anal ring flew apart as the Master rammed his shaft inside right after the head. It felt like someone had held a sharp knife over a flame until it glowed and then stuck it inside me.

But then I felt something else. There was a warming that was starting to occur even though he was still pushing himself inside me. It was the result of our skins touching for so long and it was happening deep inside my ass. The warmth had a very calming effect on me and I found myself relaxing despite the pain.

"Very impressive, Dart," Master groaned from behind me. "You've almost taken half of me and I feel like you could still take more."

"Give it all to me, Master," I moaned as I tried to hold myself steady as the big man assaulted my ass from behind.

He chuckled and said, "Well, let's not get so ahead of ourselves, little one. You may have an impressive ass, but to be able to take all of my big cock in your first try would be crazy."

"My ass is yours, Master. It belongs to you. Make it do what you want it to do," I said.

He growled. "I like to hear that." He grabbed my shoulders with his rough hands and pulled back on me as he continued to push his manhood inside me. It was the most exciting sexual experience I had ever had in my young life.

"Goddamn!" the Master grunted. "Almost three-quarters of the way."

That's when I knew that I was going to be able to take him. The pain was still there and still intense, but the warming had started to turn to pleasure and I wanted it all the way inside me. And the only way to get that was to let the big man with the giant play stick inside — all the way inside.

I relaxed and with one arm, reached back and grabbed his tremendously thick thigh and pulled it toward me. I felt him push with one last effort and felt his cock sink to a new depth inside me where no man has ever been before. He made a grunting sound of satisfaction while I released a sound of relief.

"What the fuck are you?" Master asked me the same question again. "Your ass is the most amazing thing I have ever felt."

But neither of us could enjoy the moment because just as he settled fully inside me up to his shorthairs two things happened. The first one was that tears streamed down my face as I realized that this man was my true Master and that his cock fit inside me like my ass was made to be around it.

The second thing to happen was an even bigger surprise—a blue ring of energy shot out into the air

The energy ring was pure light and beautiful to behold as it slowly formed a glowing band around the two of us on that bed. It started to move further away from us and pick up speed. I twisted my neck to look up at the man that I now knew was my true Master and he was staring at the circle of light in bewilderment.

The blue light circle suddenly disappeared through the walls of the cabin but there was a hazy blueish fog left behind. Master and I both stared at the fog because it seemed to be moving of its own accord. The blue fog swirled and rose, seeming to form something.

I was very aware of Master's rock-hard cock pulsating and throbbing inside me like a ticking time bomb. He had already emptied his nuts once, so the fact that he was so ready to go again was more than impressive.

The blue swirling smoke soon formed into the figure of a man. The figure moved toward us. I looked up at the Coven Master who still wore a look of shock. When I looked back at the swirling smoke figure, its features had formed and I thought I recognized it.

"Dad?"

I'm not sure which startled the Master more—me talking to the man formed of smoke or the fact that I thought it was my father. He bent over me and twisted my face toward his with both hands.

"You can do magic?" he asked forcibly.

"Not that I am aware, Master."

"This is your father?" he asked, indicating the smoke form with a quick jerk of his head.

"I think so. It reminds me of him, but it's been years since I have seen him."

"I would normally have to mix a potion in order to conjure a phantasm such as this," the big man fucking me said almost to himself.

"Gage?" the smoky figure asked. The voice that came from the unnatural man was not my father's, but I could hear him in it.

My heart leapt just like it had on the day I was rescued from the mining camp. "Dad, can you hear me?"

"Yes, I can hear you. Where are you, Gage?

The coven Master was amazed. "This is not a phantasm. This is astral projection. It's never even been attempted by anyone but an elder before." He looked down at me and asked, "How are you doing this?"

"We are doing it, Master. You and I together." I turned toward my father and said, "Dad, I'm safe. I'm going to get to come home and see you soon."

"Who is that with you, Gage?" he asked with suspicion.

"This is my Master, Dad."

"The one who took you?" he asked.

"No, the one who saved me."

Chapter Six

Part of a journal entry in the Trad Grimoud written by the Coven Master the next day, the fourth of April, two thousand nineteen.

We held our consecration ceremony tonight with the five marked men who were rescued in Russia two nights ago.

Sqo- rescued from the Polanari Military Base

Teo- rescued from the Polanari Military Base

Tomcjk- rescued from the Polanari Military Base

Pavan- rescued from the Polanari Military Base

Drotik- rescued from the Migidarian Mine

I was afraid that my symptoms would interfere with the ceremony, but I was delighted that the strange vibrations I was experiencing ceased upon my entry into the camp.

When the gang had assembled and the ceremony was about to begin, I walked through the woods toward the compass round and felt a pull. It got stronger as I got closer. I immediately thought it was the work of a talisman — a particularly powerful one that was able to penetrate my wards.

Once at the compass round, I could identify the man whom I was being drawn to — the marked man, Drotik. I had him searched and examined, but there was no talisman. I confronted the man and he said things to me that instantly told me that he was more aware of what was happening between the two of us than I had been. This man requires closer examination.

I stared in disbelief at the figure of my father, made only of smoke. My Master had his huge horse cock firmly planted inside me and now we were both seeing and hearing things that were beyond rational explanation. As if a man formed out of blue smoke wasn't odd enough, I was also having a conversation with it.

Suddenly, the door to the cabin burst open as if it had been shot open by a battering ram. I turned to see three of the warlocks rush into the bedroom led by Sloven.

"Master, are you okay?" he quickly asked when he saw us obviously in the act of fucking.

I turned back to the figure of my father made of smoke and saw that it was completely gone. Looking up, I was able to see the last feint trace of blue smoke as it dissipated into thin air.

"Does it look like I'm not doing okay, Sloven?" the Master answered angrily. His cock jerked and throbbed inside me, but he never released his firm grip on my hips.

"No, Master, but we saw an energy ring expand from the house and thought—"

"Thought what?" Master demanded. He took a deep breath and said more calmly, "I would really love to hear your thoughts on the matter, Slo, but right now I need to fuck this fine piece of ass that I find myself in. So, can you fellas wait for us in the circle and we will be out shortly. I will explain everything that I can to you at that time."

"Shortly, Master?" I asked with a smirk.

"In a while, Sloven," he corrected himself. "Now, go!"

The three warlocks slowly left the cabin, still looking around for something out of place.

Once the door was shut, I looked up at the Master and asked, "What do you think—"

The Master slapped a big meaty hand over my mouth while I was in mid-question. "I'm going to need you to be quiet for me, Dart. We can talk later, but right now, I'm going to fuck the shit out of this tight ass of yours."

I kept quiet and let him do his thing. He knew what we needed, because I was soon so caught up in the fuck that I was glad that I could just hang my head and pant rather than talk. I had been fucked by hundreds of men over the last four years, but this was something different.

Master was an unbelievable lover. He fucked with all the skill and finesse of a porn star and wielded that giant sword of his like he was Marshone from *The Walking Dead*. It was an impressive fuck that left me exhausted and more sore than I had ever been before. My asshole felt like it had been cut apart and then set on fire, but there was an itch deep inside my ass that felt like it had been scratched for the first time ever, giving me true relief.

The coven Master showed off a variety of positions for me during the fuck, but all from behind—he fucked me deep as he lay across my back, he held onto my shoulders and pulled my back into a crescent shape, he held onto my hips moving my ass back and forth over his big rod, and he hunched over me and fucked down into my sore hole. It was obvious to me that he had a lot of practice fucking, so I immediately began to worry about how I would stack up with the others who he had practiced with. In the back of my mind, I could still hear the Servant Stephan telling me that Master would get bored of me and move on.

The only thing that could have made this fuck better was if I could have watched the big man destroying my ass instead of just experiencing it. That thought soon left my mind, because I realized that my cock was getting ready to burst with my orgasm. I knew my prick was rock-hard while the Master was fucking me, but I was shocked when I felt the sensation in my balls that signaled their release.

No man had ever made me come just by fucking me

without me even touching my prick, but this one was getting ready to set the standard. Master fucked into me so hard that I felt like I couldn't stop myself. He was a grunting warrior behind me and I was his faithful horse under him. We were both sweating and heading to the same place like a runaway train headed into a tunnel at top speed.

"I'm going to cum, Master," I moaned softly to him. He had said that he needed me to be quiet, but I felt like he might want to know this information. Or at least, I hoped so.

"Come!" he commanded as he pulled my chest up to his.

The touch of my sweaty back with his muscled and sweaty chest was the final straw. My piss vent opened and I thrust my cock forward, releasing strand after strand of steaming spunk into the air.

Master continued to pump his big dick into me even as I was coming and that just seemed to pump the jizz out of my cock even more. I moaned as his hot hands roamed over my chest and neck. His smell was so intense now. I breathed in deeply trying to fill myself with the smell of flowering honeysuckle and masculine sweat.

My climax had accomplished two things—giving me my release and giving the Master a tighter target to fuck into. As soon as I began pumping cum out of my cock, my ass muscles clamped down on his thick cock and my anal ring threatened to strangle the massive beast.

"Goddamn!" the Master groaned through clenched teeth. "I didn't think this sweet hole of yours could get any tighter, but you just keep surprising me, little one."

"I'm yours, Master. I will always give you what you need."

"Fucking right, you will. This ass belongs to me now."

"Mark it as yours, Master."

He grunted behind me as he thrust the last few times deep inside me. When the Master finally lost his shit, he pushed himself into me to his absolute limit and roared with his release.

His hot spunk flooded my bowels and filled me completely. I just happened to be watching my hand, when a wart that had been there for years suddenly shrunk down into my skin and disappeared.

Holy fuck! What was this man doing to me?

"Fuck me!" the big warlock said as he wrapped me in both arms and pressed his chest to mine. He was breathing hard. "I wish we had time to do that like six more times," he said as his hips began to undulate, causing his cock to move back and forth inside me again.

I felt the cum drilled out of my ass as it began to run down onto my sweaty legs. *Six more times? This man's stamina was amazing . . .*

"I don't want the others to think that I am manipulating your time, Master," I finally said.

"Like hell, you don't," he said with a snort. "You would keep me here between your magical legs all night regardless of how many people waited on us if you wanted to."

*I want to, Master, trust me . . ."*I am yours to command, Master, not the other way around," I stated simply.

"You would do well to remember that, little one," he said as he released me and lifted off of me. He ever so slowly pulled his still throbbing cock out of my ass and brought it to my mouth.

I hated the feeling of a NOMAR pulling his cock out of my ass after an especially hard fuck. There were not many things in the world that were as depressing as that feeling of emptiness that followed.

I sucked and cleaned the Master's tremendous stallion and felt it harden and spark inside my mouth. I looked up at him while his cock was punching into the back of my throat and nearly choked. In my experience, looking up at a man while my mouth was full of his manhood was a sure-fire way to get a reaction out of him, but this time it was me that reacted.

"What?" he asked.

"Master, look . . ." I pointed to the mirror above the dresser.

He turned and stepped up to the mirror. Not only were his muscles totally ripped and defined like mine were since I had swallowed his cum, but now his massive chest was covered in black man-fur. His long dark hair had shortened and was now spiky and where his face had been covered with a full black beard, now there was the dark stubble of a five o'clock shadow.

"Holy fuck!" he said as he ran his hand over his hair and jawline. He flexed his massive biceps in front of the mirror which practically made me drool. I was also getting my first look at his amazing ass.

"Look what you are doing to me, little one," he said, turning toward me.

"You are hot as fuck, Master," I said, my voice heady with lust.

"This is the way you like me?" he asked.

"I like you any way, Master, but yes, I think the magic upgraded you for me," I told him with a wink.

"Huh," he said as he looked at his new self in the mirror.

"We seem to be good for each other, Master."

"Thank you for that fuck, Dart. I still don't understand what is happening or who you are, but I think we will figure it out."

"Thank you, Master."

"I meant what I said. We will talk later tonight and I will let you have whatever you want, if you will agree to be mine." He struggled getting his new thigh muscles into his jeans, but finally was able to accomplish the deed.

"Thank you, Master." I tried to stand, but found it to be

too painful.

"Let me," he said as he reached down and cradled me in his arms. The skin of his chest sparked against my bare arm, but it soon turned warm so I lay my head against his furry chest and let him carry me.

I could feel his cum dripping out of my sloppy ass. "Should I clean myself up before I go back out there, Master?" I asked, indicating my dripping ass with one hand.

"No. I want them all to see my cum dripping out of you." He turned off the lights in the cabin and shut the door with a wave of his hand.

We walked back to the fire circle in silence. He carried me to my position on the pentagram and lowered me down amid gasps and whispers from all of the others. I had never felt closer to someone in my whole life.

As I knelt on the point of the star, I was acutely aware that all of the eyes in the circle were glued to the two of us. I made sure that as I knelt I didn't let my sore ass touch my heels behind me. My cock was as hard as it could get.

Master stood in front of me but moved back closer to the fire. I noticed that his big cock was just as hard as it had been in the cabin despite having just lost his shit twice in the last hour. His mighty python fought hard against the denim fabric of his jeans.

Master stared at me with his dark eyes, "Marked man known as Dart. Do you accept the employment opportunity that the Vrajitor has offered you? Will you become their Servant and serve them faithfully? Will you give of your body in return for riches?"

"I accept, Master." I saw my man visibly relax in front of me.

"Excellent," he said with a huge sigh of relief.

Master turned away from me and moved around the circle. It was the first time that we had been separated since returning to the fire. I saw the physical transformation in his body at the same time that I felt mine. It suddenly felt like my muscles had been deflated and it was cool to see Master's smooth chest return even as his long hair extended down his back.

Master turned toward me and looked across the fire at me. He saw that I had changed, so I nodded to him now in his original form to let him know that it was okay. "Welcome, new members of the Vrajitori."

"Sain baculum," the assembled men said in unison.

I shot a quick glance at Sqo next to me in the circle. He returned a look that I read as *What the fuck is going on?* I raised my shoulders to let him know that I wasn't quite sure.

Master raised his voice and announced, "These men need to be aspergered. We will now hold the cleansing ceremony."

He walked up to Teo and said his name. The Master moved onto the next one of us and said his name. He made his way around the circle saying each one of our names until he was right in front of me—hairy chest and short cropped hair. We both had changed to our better forms.

I smiled up at the Master and he looked down at me with such lust that my cock felt like it would explode. His was always hard, even with his jeans on. I was in awe of his stamina, his body, his cock, and his control over me.

"Brothers, come into the circle," he commanded. While the warlocks made their way around the fire, Master explained, "Marked men, we will now spray you with our most precious gift—our seed, our life force, our future, our energy. This spraying of our energy will cleanse you and make you one of us."

The warlocks joined their Master in the circle facing us—each one of them more spectacular than the next. The warlocks divided themselves around the four of us marked men and began to take their clothes off.

Master addressed his gang once they were completely naked. At first, it was hard to focus on him once I saw that all of the warlocks were beautifully hung and all were hard as steel girders, but none of them compared to the Master, so my eyes eventually returned to him.

His voice bellowed out in the clearing, "No one asperges Dart. Do I make myself clear?" The Master's tone conveyed that he was not to be fucked with on this issue.

"Yes, Master," all of the men replied. The five men who had been huddled around me moved away toward my three Russian friends.

"You are one of us now," the Master said loudly as he began to jack his huge cock right in front of me.

The rest of the gang followed the coven Master's lead and began to stroke their organs until they reached their release. They came in a spectacular fireworks display of white cum splashing all over the Russian marked men's faces.

The Master joined the other warlocks in their release, his big hand wrapped around his thick shaft. He held it steady as he erupted with his climax and released his load onto my face. His back arched as he pumped strand after strand of hot cum onto me.

I closed my eyes and opened my mouth, hoping to catch as much of the Master's essence as possible. I felt a little guilty that I wasn't getting the full bukkake that the others were, but I loved that the Master was claiming me in front of all the others.

The Master placed his fat cock onto my face, used it to sweep some of his cum into my mouth, and said, "You are us."

I opened my eyes just in time to see the other warlocks do and say the same thing. Once everyone was finished, Master turned to address the assembled men.

"Dart and I will finish our negotiation tonight. He will sleep with me when we are finished. Sloven, you will be responsible for negotiating with the others in my absence."

I felt the judgements and saw the looks of shock on the others' faces, especially the Servants. But none of that mattered because the Master wanted to sleep with me tonight and that's all that mattered to me.

CHAPTER SEVEN

Part of a journal entry written by the Vrajitor Servant, Dart, on the morning of April the fourth, two thousand nineteen.

Tonight, I met the most amazing man that I have ever encountered. He had a physical effect on me – my body in tune with his every movement. He had an emotional effect on me – my emotions directly linked to his. He had a sexual effect on me – my ass and mouth never received a fucking like the one he had just given me.

I have not informed him yet, but I am pretty sure that he is my true Master. Every marked boy has heard the stories—marked men who are perfectly paired with a NOMAR in every way. The tellers of the true Master stories always said that there was only one set and never another. I thought that the stories were just urban legend created to make marked men constantly fuck with NOMARs to try to find their true Master. But now I was sure that there is such a thing, and I was positive that the coven Master was him for me.

I had just met the man less than two hours ago, but I had never had a connection like that before. Granted that I had been held hostage and forced to fuck miners for the last four years, but I still knew what I was experiencing was something unique and not just different.

This man had the body of a Greek God and the looks of a movie star. He was rugged, smart, and funny – a real man's man. But what I liked best about him was his confidence and his swagger. I could tell that he was caring and compassionate, but above all he was dominant. I never believed that I would ever make a good submissive, but I would give it a hella shot for this man. Nothing turned me on like the Master dominating me.

And the Master was most dominant when he was fucking. I can attest to that and he had only fucked me once. This man was the one for me and I didn't even know his name . . .

The coven Master had just announced to his gang that he was going to finish the night negotiating with me. And it didn't seem to be sitting so well with them.

Sloven was the first warlock to speak. "Master?" I recognized that he was speaking Witchspeak, but I could easily understand it.

The Master answered in Witchspeak. "You heard me, Sloven. I will spend the night with Dart after I finish his negotiation. You will handle the rest."

"That's not the way we usually do it, Master," Sloven said.

"This is not the usual negotiation, Sloven. You will be fine with those three. I will take this more complicated one," the Master said while still staring at me lustfully. "There is nothing complicated about his hole though, Slo. It is pure pleasure being inside him."

I blushed furiously, revealing that I could understand what they were saying. Master cocked his head to the side and stared at me even harder with a curious look on his face.

Sloven moved over to stand beside the Master. He leaned in where only the three of us could hear him and said, "Master, do you realize that you are changing physically when you are near him?"

"Yes, Slo. I appreciate your concern for me. We have a lot to discuss."

"Perhaps now would be a good time to talk, Master," Sloven suggested.

The Master took his gaze off of me for the first time since

Sloven had come over. He looked at his fellow warlock and seemed to be studying him for a minute. "Okay, Sloven. Let's go talk. The rest of you get these men cleaned up," he commanded the others.

I watched in fascination as the two big warlocks moved off to the side of the clearing. Some of the other warlocks were carrying out a big cooler of water and a basket of towels. The Master walked over to where the cooler was, cupped his hand, and poured water into his palm. He rejoined Sloven and he placed his palm into the water as they both bent their heads.

An amazing ball of light appeared in the darkened forest above Master and his friend's head. It slowly started to melt like molton glass around them. By the time that the liquid glass hit the forest floor, I saw that it was a glass cage that radiated its own light. Master held up his hand inside the cage and the glass suddenly frosted, keeping me from seeing anything more.

When I turned back to the circle, I was surrounded. Everyone else was standing right in front of me. One of the warlocks offered me a hand and I gingerly stood up as he handed me a wet towel. I covered my shock at seeing them all by wiping my face slowly.

"What the fuck did you say to him in that cabin?" Stephan demanded to know.

"The Master fucked him," one of the warlocks said with a grin on his face.

"And obviously liked it," another one said.

"Impossible," Stephan said. "The Master doesn't go back to the same hole again so soon. And he has never slept with one of us before." If the Servant could have shot fire through his eyes at me, he would have.

"He's going to this time," I smirked as I grabbed a dry towel from another warlock and dabbed my face.

"Why did the Master carry him out of the cabin?" one of the warlocks asked another one.

"C'mon, Pacquin, you've seen the size of the Master's cock. Imagine walking after having that thing pounded inside you," the other one answered.

"Oh, right," the one called Pacquin said.

"You must have done something to him or told him something," Stephan said, searching.

"Who cares?" one of the older warlocks asked. "I'm glad for the Master if he has found a hole that he likes, but what I am curious about is the unusual magic that is happening between the two of them."

"Yeah," a younger warlock agreed. "How do you do that spell where you change your look when you two are near each other?"

"And what was that blue energy ring that left the cabin when the Master was fucking you?" another one asked.

"I'm not sure that we have the answers to your questions yet," I said carefully.

"We?" Stephan repeated in disgust.

"Yes, we." The Master's deep voice boomed right behind me into the group of men. He moved right beside me and put a muscled arm around my waist. "Dart and I will continue to try to solve those mysteries while we negotiate his salary."

"Yes, Master," they all said as they bowed their heads to him.

"Sloven is in charge of the rest," the Master informed the crowd as he easily bent over and picked me up into his arms. "Tomorrow night is the black moon and we have great work to do, so get a lot of rest and be at your best."

"Yes, Master."

I tried not to look smug when I stared at Stephan, but I knew that it was written all over my face. I did not care for the head Servant and his major attitude. I finally leaned my head back onto the Master's furry chest. urning around, he walked through the woods with me.

We did not go to a near-by cabin this time but to a much bigger cabin on the far side of the camp. The Master waved open the door, and I instantly knew from the smell that this was his cabin. Another wave of his hand turned on the lamps. Everything in this cabin smelled like him and it made my prick harder than it already was.

The small kitchen was filled with hanging herbs and the furniture was simple but good quality, most of it leather. The Master gently put me down in one of the leather chairs in the living room and lit a fire in the fireplace with another wave of his hand.

"Would you like a drink, little one?"

"Yes, Master."

"Good. I plan on keeping you mounted on my big cock for most of the night, so a drink will do you good. What would you like to have?"

His words made my balls smolder with desire, but he said them with such frankness that I wasn't sure he knew what he was doing to me. "Whatever you are having is fine with me, Master."

"I'm having some ale, little one."

I nodded to him that I was fine with that. The Master moved into the kitchen and returned with two mugs of dark brown ale. He handed me one and sat the other on the mantle.

He challenged me, "Would you like to talk now, little one, or do you need a hard fucking first?"

"I would like to have your giant baby-maker inside me when we talk, Master. Do you think you could wait to fuck me with it after we finish talking or will that be too difficult for you?" I asked, challenging him back.

The big man growled at me and said, "When you belong to me, I will not allow you to say things like that to me, little one."

When I belong to you? I swallowed hard and stared into his dark eyes.

"Perhaps if you suck me off first, I will be able to control myself once I'm inside that sweet hole of yours," he suggested with a raised eyebrow.

"And so the negotiations begin . . ." I said as I slid off the front of the chair onto my knees.

"You are a smart man, Dart," the Master said as he unbuttoned his jeans and peeled them off his even-more muscular thighs.

"You are my Master," I said as I reached out and pulled his dick toward my hot mouth. Electric sparks exploded between my hand and the skin of his cock. I licked my lips as I anticipated having a delicious mouthful of the Master's manhood.

"You can say that again," he growled as he stepped forward and shoved several more inches of himself inside me.

Actually, I can't, Master. My mouth is kinda full . . .

The Master was already so hard that I had to lift myself up higher in order to bend his steel beam between my lips. He was already leaking pre-cum and I was a whore making sure that I didn't miss a single drop of it. I sucked on his fat joint with long drawing pulls that hollowed out my cheeks.

"Goddamn!" Master said through gritted teeth as he grabbed each side of my head and held me tight. He proceeded to face fuck me until he reached his release.

Master let go of the sides of my head as he arched his back and exploded with his climax. I held onto his prick and backed it out of my mouth so that he could fill me with his delicious cream. Swallowing fast, I kept up with his flow until he subsided and then stopped.

I ran my thumb up the thick bottom vein of his shaft from

root to tip coaxing more pearls of cum from his fuck stick. I sucked each one of them off his cum vent as soon as they appeared.

"You are really good at that, little one," he said with a voice still colored with lust.

"Your big cock inspires me, Master."

"I'm going to be inspired by your ass next," he promised me.

"I look forward to it," I said with a smirk as I looked up at him.

"I want you right here by the fire," he told me as he handed me my glass of ale.

I drank deeply as he moved his glass to the floor and then also an ashtray. I hated cigarette smoking, but fortunately for me I saw him grab a fat cigar from a box on the mantle.

"You don't mind if I smoke, do you?" he asked holding the cigar out.

"No, Master."

"Good. When you belong to me, I will not care whether you mind or not. Would you like one?"

"No, thank you, Master."

He sat down on the carpet facing the fire and patted his lap. "It is time to talk, little one."

"May I lube your tremendous cock, Master?"

His tone smoldered as he answered, "You may, little one. You will find it in the bedroom. Lube my cock well, because it will be inside you for the rest of the night."

"Yes, Master," I said as I hustled to the bedroom. I found the lube on the nightstand, grabbed it, and was quickly back.

I lubed up the massive pole that I would soon be sitting on with as much care as was possible. "You do that with such affection, little one," the Master remarked.

I looked up into his face while my hands still worked his pole, "It is very important to me, Master."

"But you just met it a few hours ago, Dart . . ."

"It belongs to me now, Master."

He chuckled and asked, "Does it now?"

I laughed with him. "I know it is probably your favorite thing, Master, but now it is mine also."

"Does that mean that your ass now belongs to me?" he asked with a smirk.

"That's exactly what it means, Master. You belong to me and I belong to you."

"Well then get my ass down onto my prick," he said with a smile right before clamping the big stogie between his teeth and lighting it.

"Yes, Master," I said grinning.

I stood above him on out-stretched legs and lowered myself down onto my knees until I was sitting on his thighs. The Master blew out a mouthful of smoke and then put his cigar in the corner of his mouth. He used his hands to position my ass above his crotch and then to feed his giant cock into my puckered hole.

"Oh, fuck!" he exclaimed as he slid his extra-large shaft into my anal channel after I squeezed it with my asshole on the way in. "What kind of spell do you put on me that makes me believe that your ass is this tight when I know that less than an hour ago, I railed you out with my big cock? You should not be this tight again so soon, little one."

"No magic, Master. It is just the way my ass is. Hence the name . . ."

The Master waited until he had pushed me completely down onto his rod before he said anything. He opened his mouth to ask me a question, but the sudden release of a blue energy ring from us stopped him short. The ring slowly hovered around us and then expanded through the walls. "Your name, Dart?"

"Are we going to act like that didn't just happen again,

Master?"

"Yes, until I can figure it out."

"Yes, Master," I said, trying to ignore the roaring pain in my asshole as it stretched to its limits and the throbbing of the Master's cock deep inside "When the Russians first got me, they immediately discovered my special skill and gave me the nickname."

"But why Dart?" he asked as he puffed on his stogie.

"The miners called me Dartboard, Master, because of the way that my ass makes every dart stick tight, no matter the shape or size. And also for the way that it rebounds back to its original shape when the dart is removed."

"I can see why they called you that, little one." He reached under my ass and lifted me up his pole before pulling me back down.

I rocked my ass back and forth to make sure that he was completely inside me. "It is a good name for me, Master."

"And what is your real name?"

"My what, Master?" I asked, panicked. I had not told anyone my real name in close to four years and no one had ever asked before.

"You heard me, little one. Don't make me repeat myself. I don't like that. What I do like is having a name that I call you that no one else uses. There is power in that and if you are going to be mine then I require it."

"Gage, Master."

"Gage," he repeated, blowing out a big plume of smoke. The Master's English was excellent, but he did have a bit of an accent when he said my name. I just happened to really like it.

"Yes, Master. And what is your name?"

He pushed my hips up his thick shaft and pulled me back down. "You will call me Master, little one."

"I already do that, Master."

"No, you call me the Master. But now you will call me Master."

I held my breath after I asked, "You want me to be your Servant, Master?" I couldn't believe that this big man wanted to be my Master. It was like a dream come true.

"I don't think I have much choice in the matter, Gage. You are mine now and there is no other way to control you than to become your Master."

"You want to control me, Master?"

"Someone has to, little one." He smirked as he held my ass up and thrust his hips up several times fast in a row.

I'm glad that you are the one, Master . . .

CHAPTER EIGHT

Part of an unofficial military report filed by the commander of the Polanari military base to his commanders at the Kremlin in Moscow filed on the fourth of April, two thousand nineteen.

On the night of April first, 2019 four of the marked men that we were holding to relieve the soldiers at the Polanari military base were found to be missing. At first inspection, it appears that they were able to get out of their locked housing unit and off of the base, but I think a closer examination is needed in this matter.

The raid on Polanari was meant to look like a group of marked men made an escape, but I am convinced that it was indeed a raid by some foreign power. There are several pieces of the puzzle that at first appear random, but when taken together they suggest a raid. These events have to be considered.

The night of the escape, not one single door was opened using security clearance and the doors remained in perfect working order afterward.

No trace of the escaped marked men has been found or heard about in Russia. How did they leave the country without there being a record?

All of the soldiers who were on patrol that night report the same exact story – a flash of light and then nothing. As far as we are able to tell, each of them have the same recollection, no matter where their duty post was located.

All of the soldiers who witnessed the flash of light have time missing from their memories. As far as we can determine, there is more than four minutes unaccounted for.

And most damning of all is the fact that a nearby mining camp has also reported that their one marked man escaped that same night. The miners who were interviewedeported the same flashes of light and missing time. The escaped marked man has also never been seen or heard from since.

My ability to think straight was truly being affected by having my Master's big fat cock firmly planted deep inside my ass. Fortunately for me, I could tell that he was struggling with the same exact issue. He just told me that he wanted to be my Master, and I was thrilled at the prospect.

I watched as my Master took a long draw from his cigar before putting it down into the ashtray. "I think I have an explanation for some of this, Master," I said as I wrapped my long arms around his thick neck and rode the gentle swells of his throbbing cock.

"I'm listening," he said after blowing his smoke out into my face.

"I think you might be my true Master, Master."

He looked at me with narrowed eyes for a couple of seconds and said, "I have considered that already."

"And you have dismissed it?" I asked.

"No, it is a viable answer. Tell me why you think I am the perfect match for you, little one." He made sure to thrust into me a couple of times for maximum effect. He picked up his ale, drank some, and then lifted the bottle to my lips.

I swallowed some beer and said, "I think it would explain the connection we have with each other, Master—like how we physically were bound to each other when we were close but apart. I feel like I can read your feelings even without seeing your face or body language sometimes."

"I agree," he said softly.

"And no one can deny that we have sexual chemistry off the charts," I said, almost panting as I bounced on his big prick.

He reached for his cigar again. "Amen to that."

"And your dick feels like it was made in the shape of my ass, Master," I added quickly.

The big man laughed and said, "It certainly does. They are like puzzle pieces that form together. You are the first man that has ever been able to take me on the first try and now the second time we fuck you are just as tight as ever for me, so your ass is truly something unique." He took a puff off of his cigar.

I blushed at his words and his intent gaze. His face was so close to mine and his body was all over and inside me. My own cock was so painfully hard and our skins were sparking with energy everywhere that we were touching. "I've never really considered myself a submissive before, Master, but your dominance over me is really exciting."

"And there is something more," he guessed when I was silent for a moment.

"You said that I needed to be controlled, Master, and I want nothing more than to be controlled by you. I want to please you from now on, and I don't care what I get out of it except that."

His mouth slowly turned into a big smile that showed all of his beautiful teeth. Master put his cigar into the ashtray without ever taking his gaze from mine. "Well, that should certainly make the negotiations go much easier."

"I will do as you command me, Master," I said as I bowed my head to him.

He lifted my chin with two rough fingers until my gaze met his. "I told you that I would give you anything you wanted and I am a man of my word, Gage. But it thrills me to no end to see you bend to my will. Trust me when I say that we will have plenty of time to experience all of each other. We will do things together that neither of us thought possible, and we will experience the ultimate pleasure of our bodies while we do it."

My mouth was suddenly very dry. "My true Master."

"My true Servant. Now, that we have that out of the way, what would you like to negotiate for?"

"Can you finish fucking me, Master? I can't even think straight anymore," I admitted.

He grinned again and said, "I certainly can finish us off, but then I'm just going to fuck you again, so I don't know whether it will help or not, little one."

"It will help, Master."

"Beg me," he ordered.

I considered him for a second. *I can play this game.* I said, "Please fuck me, Master. I need it so bad. You are the only one that can give me what I need and I need it right now."

"You want this big cock that's up inside you?" he asked, his voice heady with lust.

"Yes, Master."

"What do you want me to do with it, little one?"

"I want you to fuck me with it, Master. Fuck me hard and fast." I didn't really have to put on a show, because I was telling the truth. I did want him to fuck me as hard and fast as he possibly could.

The man who I now considered my true Master smiled at me and said, "I will grant your wish, little one, as long as you will grant me a wish of my own later."

"Agreed, Master." I moaned. At this point, I needed to be fucked so badly that I might have agreed to anything. And there was nothing I could think of that I would not do for him.

The coven Master held me suspended above his crotch as his legs and hips bounced up and down below me. This caused his big cock to repeatedly thrust into me at a high rate of speed. It felt like my asshole was being set on fire, but

Master was scratching the itch deep inside me that I needed him to.

"I'm coming, Master," I groaned behind closed eyelids. This man did things to me that I assumed were not possible.

"Me too, Gage." He moaned as we both hit our releases within seconds of each other.

Master pumped my sore ass full of his hot discharge while I sprayed mine all over our two chests. I loved seeing his dark chest hair matted with my stark white cum. The firelight made everything look dreamier than it probably was.

We both were breathing hard and holding onto each other as we recovered from our orgasm. It was heaven holding onto his massive biceps and having his big prick inside me at the same time—the feeling was indescribable. I felt closer to him than I had felt to anyone maybe ever.

I released his arms and leaned back so that I could look at my new Master. He was so handsome that I couldn't believe he was mine.

"What?" he asked as he put his knees up and laid his arms across them.

"Master!" I said suddenly.

"What?" he asked again.

"Your cigar," I said pointing.

Master was still clenching his cigar between his fingers. He lifted his hand and the cigar sparkled in the firelight. We both stared at the golden cigar in the same half-smoked shape it was in when I watched him puff on it.

"How?" he asked, his eyes flicked from the piece of gold in his hand to my face.

"I don't know, Master. Were you holding onto it when we both lost our shit?"

Master narrowed his eyes, looked at the gold nugget again and said, "Yes, why?"

"Last time we fucked, we conjured my father and this time maybe we turned the cigar to gold," I hypothesized.

"That's alchemy. It's a very complex spell, Gage."

"We better do it again and see if something else happens this time," I said with a raised eyebrow.

"For the sake of experimentation?" Master asked with a smirk. His cock was still hard and throbbing inside me.

"Yes, Master."

"Before we finish our negotiations?" he asked.

"They are pretty much done, Master. You have already agreed to give me whatever I want, so what more is there?"

The big man whose lap I was sitting on laughed out loud, causing me to shake. "And what is it that you want, my little one?"

"I want to go visit my father." I saw the look of mirth leave my Master's face immediately. I quickly added, "Just to visit, Master, for a little while."

"I will come with you," he immediately told me.

"Yes," I said with sudden excitement. "But I don't even think that I can afford my way home, Master."

"Don't worry, little one. I have more than enough money for both of us. Besides, this will probably pay for our way," he said as he held up the fat cigar made of gold.

"We better make something else, then, to make sure that we have extra spending money for our trip, Master."

"So eager, aren't you, little one?"

I admitted, "I can't seem to get enough of you, Master."

"It's only been a day," he said with a chuckle.

I blushed furiously, knowing that he was onto me. "Don't worry, Gage, I feel the same way. And there is nothing else that you want from me?"

"I just want you, Master."

"You got me, but there is nothing else?"

"No, Master."

He smiled and said, "You will want for nothing, little one. I will shower you with all of my attention."

"I'm afraid that will not go over very well with the others . . ."

"Nothing about you has gone over well with them. They will just have to deal with it." He smiled a devilish grin and asked, "What shall we try to transform next?"

"How about the ale bottle, Master?" I asked as I took a swig.

"No. It has to be something natural, I think," he answered me as he started to look around. When he turned back toward me, he wore a mischievous grin.

"What?"

He growled.

"What, Master?" I quickly added.

"I have an idea," he told me as he bent his lower legs behind him and rolled me onto my back.

I was now lying on the thick rug in front of the fire and my Master still had me impaled on his beautiful cock. He knelt between my legs before reaching over and grabbing a vase of herbs off of one of the tables.

"Hemlock," he told me as he pulled the herbs out of the vase.

"Isn't that poisonous, Master?"

He raised an eyebrow and asked, "Oh, so somebody knows about their plants, do they?"

I nodded as I felt his cock expand inside me again.

"Yes, it is poisonous, but I want to use the water. Now, hold still, little one."

I watched in fascination as the big man deftly poured water from the vase onto my stomach. When he was satisfied, he carefully put the vase back and put the hemlock plants back into it.

Master turned to me, checked my stomach, and put each

of my ankles on the top of his collarbone. "I'm going to fuck you hard again, Gage, and we will see what happens."

"Yes, Master." *We could experiment all night long as far as I care. This is one of my favorite positions and the only thing left to do is to have Master fucking rail me out while he has me bent in half.*

Master leaned forward over me, bending me like a taco shell. He planted his big hands on either side of my shoulders and held himself above me with his massive biceps locked in place like marble columns on a Roman temple. I had never been dominated by someone like I was by this man and it turned me on like crazy.

And then he started to fuck me. It was a slow gentle grind at first—my Master making sure that he gave me every inch of his long dick before pulling all the way out and pushing it in again. It was an amazing feeling with me worrying each time that he pulled out if my anal ring would stretch wide enough to take him back again.

"Fuck! How in the hell do you stay so tight?" he asked without interrupting his slow methodical fuck.

"I want to be tight for you every time, Master," I told him as I put my hands on his broad shoulders and hung onto him.

"It has been, each and every time." He grunted as he picked up speed and began to really fuck me. Master was careful to not let the phlange of his beautiful cock leave my ass now so that his thrusts could come faster and with more force than before. I was grateful that my asshole stayed constantly stretched out which gave me more pleasure than I had ever had before.

We both stayed silent as the coven Master put on a spectacular show of fucking and I rode his thrusts to another climax. The fire had warmed both of our skins to an amazing level and my nostrils were full of his masculine smell. This man was having some kind of effect on me and I was living for it. As soon as my prick pumped all of its seed onto my chest, I clamped down onto his big prick with the muscles in my ass.

"That's the shit right there," my Master said through clenched teeth. His speed and depth of thrust were at the max and he was just about ready to explode. He kept thrusting until he lost his shit.

"Fuuuuuccccckkkkkk!" he howled as his back arched and his prick erupted inside me.

I held onto his sweaty back as Master breathed like a horse after a long gallop. I gently massaged and caressed his powerful muscles as he regained himself. I loved his weight on top of me, pressing me down like I was in a giant hairy Panini machine.

The coven Master finally was able to lift himself off of me. He stared down at me. "I don't know what the fuck you are or what you are doing to me, but I don't really care if that's how this is going to go."

I chuckled and agreed with him.

We were finally able to break our gazes away from each other as Master pulled himself back to a kneeling position. His hairy stomach separated from mine and I saw something glisten between. I had already forgotten about our little experiment.

Master reached down and pried something out of my belly button. It was hard and shiny. He pulled it up to where the firelight could play on it and it looked other-worldly like a small jellyfish.

"What is it, Master?"

"It's the water from the vase," he said as he inspected it. "It's made of silver now."

"Wow."

Master looked at me oddly for a second and then grinned. "Shall we go to my bed and see what else we can do?"

"I am yours to command, my Master."
He growled, "Fucking right, you are."
And you are mine, Master . . .

CHAPTER NINE

Part of a journal entry by the Servant, Gage, that he wrote the day after his cleansing ceremony on the sixth of April, two thousand nineteen.

I was fortunate to have my journals with me when I was rescued, so I will continue to write in them about my experiences. And the past two days have been just that – experiences.

It started with my very unusual rescue from the mining camp, continued to a day of rest at my rescuers' camp that wasn't exactly normal, and then culminated with the entrance of the coven Master. The big dark coven Master has also turned out to be my true Master.

I was pretty sure that he was my true Master and then we fucked and I knew for sure. He is unlike anyone that I have ever met before. We had a very frank discussion about it, while his giant cock was buried to the hilt inside my ass, and he asked me to become his Servant.

I accepted immediately and afterward I negotiated about when I could go visit my father. Master had agreed for the visit and insisted that he would accompany me on my trip. I was thrilled about that.

Every time that Master enters me, a blue ring of energy shoots into space from the point of our coupling. The first time that we fucked, the blue energy took the form of my father and I was able to have an actual conversation with him. Master was amazed at this magic and said that only a few people in history knew how to accomplish it.

The second time that we fucked, the blue ring just hovered and then disappeared, but what Master and I discovered later was that it had made a change in our environment. My Master was growing a lot of herbs and plants in his house for use in potions and spells. After fucking, we discovered that the plants were all in full bloom, some of them healthier than they ever had been. The dried ones were now fully alive again and each plant had doubled in size. Master was truly bewildered by the rejuvenation spell.

We uncoupled and he fucked me again in his bedroom that night. The blue energy this time made a projection of the heavens on the darkened bedroom ceiling that we both stared at as we fucked. It was beautiful and gave just enough light for me to watch my handsome Master tearing me up.

True to my Master's word, he had kept me impaled on his big cock for most of the night and now in the morning, I was sore as hell. I wasn't even sure if I would be able to walk, but he assured me that I would be able to.

Master left the bedroom and returned with several different branches of plants which he placed on the bed. The only one I recognized was mint. He also carried a heavy mortar and pestle which he also placed on the bed.

"Lift your legs, little one," he commanded.

I did, immediately feeling the effects of being completely fucked last night. I stared in wonder at my Master as he reached over to me and stuck two of his big fingers into my ass and dug around. A wonderful mixture of pleasure and pain filled me, but the sharp pain threatened to win this round.

He pulled his fingers out and lowered my legs. "Go get cleaned up, Gage, and when you finish, I will have completed this poultice." He wiped cum off of his fingers into the mortar. "It will make you feel much better."

Sure enough, after showering, I had no sooner gotten onto all fours on the bed that I started feeling better. Master immediately applied the poultice to my asshole and it was like taking a magic wand and waving it over my butt.

"Much better, Master, thank you."

"I'm going to jump in the shower and then we will go eat," he told me. "You are welcome to look around the house, but do not leave it. Do I make myself clear?"

"Yes, Master. Are there clothes for me to wear?" I asked without even thinking about it.

"If I want you to wear clothing, I will provide it for you," he said evenly as he walked into the bathroom and shut the door.

"Yikes!" I said aloud in the empty cottage as I looked around.

I fingered the plants in the kitchen. They looked a lot bigger and bushier than when I first walked into Master's cabin, but maybe I just hadn't really been that observant before. My new Master had a lot of books in the living room—he was obviously very well-read, judging from the worn spines and covers.

I looked up from the book cover that I was reading and saw my Master standing completely naked in the doorway to the bedroom. He had a wet towel in his hand.

"You are a reader, little one?" he asked huskily.

"Yes, Master," I answered him, realizing too late that I was staring and drooling at him.

"Close your mouth, Gage. We have work to do," he said mysteriously as he disappeared back into the bedroom.

Work?

I was still taxing my brain to figure out what my new Master was talking about when he appeared behind me. I was standing in front of a shelving unit positioned in front of a window. On the shelves were the most amazingly beautiful crystals. It could not hold my fascination compared to what I felt for the man behind me. His nearness was intoxicating to me just like the best high I could possibly imagine.

"Master," I said with a huge sigh without even turning around.

"Gage, it is time to go," he said spinning me around. I saw that he was wearing a red and black plaid shirt over jeans and construction boots. He looked like a big yummy lumberjack. "We will eat something and then we will meet with the other senior members of my gang."

I nodded my head and followed him to the door, super-aware that I was going to do these things completely naked. I wanted him to be my Master and I loved his domination over me. Therefore, I had to suck it up and deal with what-ever decisions he made for me.

It gave me a certain thrill to walk out of the cottage be-hind my Master, regardless of my nakedness. He was the big man in charge and I belonged to him. I was very proud of that fact. It was hard for me to keep the grin off my face when the others we ran into stopped and bowed to him.

Master walked me toward the dining hall and held the door for me. I nodded to thank him as I stepped into the room and came to a dead stop. Every table held at least six men and the room was crowded. All conversations stopped and they all faced me when I entered. Suddenly, I was not so proud anymore.

The coven Master brushed by me and started greeting the other men. I noticed right away that the marked men were wearing clothing just like the warlocks and that made me feel totally different.

"How was your night of negotiation?" one of the war-locks asked my Master.

He turned around and stared at me with his dark eyes. "It was quite rewarding. Wasn't it, Dart?"

This is the first time since yesterday that he has called me by that name. I loved that he was going to call me one thing in public and another in private. It gave our relationship a cer-tain intimacy that I had never experienced before.

"Yes, Master. I was constantly being rewarded."

The men at the table all laughed and Master slapped some of them on the backs as he moved on through the tables. I could smell the food in front of us and my stomach growled impatiently.

Master stopped at the last table. Sloven was seated at this table with the two warlocks who had rescued me from the mining camp. Unfortunately, the disagreeable Servant Stephan was also seated at the table. He gave me a glare as I stood beside my Master.

"Sloven," the coven Master's deep voice bellowed in the large room, "Dart and I are going to eat and then I would like to meet with you and the other senior leadership. Stay around after everyone leaves."

Sloven shot a quick glance at me and said, "Yes, Master."

"Very good," Master said to the table. He put a big muscled arm around my back and nudged me forward toward the food. "Get us some food, little one," he commanded me.

I went to the buffet table and picked up two plates. There were a lot of choices of breakfast foods and I wasn't sure what Master liked and what he didn't. I loaded his plate down with almost everything and only put the stuff on my plate that I liked.

As I spooned fruit onto my pancakes, I watched Master continuing to manipulate the crowd. I was very aware that he was also constantly watching me. When I was finally satisfied with the amount of food that I had gathered, I turned to see that my Master had taken a seat at one of the tables recently vacated.

I carried both plates over to the table and sat the full one down in front of my Master. He was talking to one of the warlocks who had approached him, so I sat down beside him.

He finished his conversation and turned to look at his

plate of food. "Coffee, Dart, coffee."

I jumped up and headed toward large silver urns across the room. Some of the warlocks and Servants were leaving the dining hall now, but I was fortunate to run into one at the coffee stand.

"Hi, I'm Dart," I said to the tall thin blond-haired warlock.

"Boris," he said. "You have been lucky to catch the Master's attention, no?"

"Yes, I have," I admitted. "Would you happen to know how he drinks his coffee?"

"Black," he immediately said.

"Thanks," I said with relief as I poured two steaming cups.

"No problem. Let me know if I can ever help you again."

"Thanks, I will," I said with genuine honesty.

"I'm sure that you will find a lot of us to be very helpful to you," he said with a smirk.

I asked, "Why's that?"

The young warlock looked at me strangely for a second and then explained, "If you have the Master's favor, then you will have a lot of influence with him. And if we have your favor, then we will have a lot of influence with him."

"I suppose that could come into play," I said, knowing that it would be politically prudent of me to keep him on the line rather than shutting him down like I wanted to. I had no intention of trying to manipulate my Master in any way except for my own means when necessary.

"Remember my name," he said with a grin before leaving.

I carried the two coffee mugs over to Master's table and immediately saw that he was eating my plate of food. He grinned up at me and asked, "You have something to say, little one?" He intentionally forked a piece of fresh pineapple and bit it, holding it between his beautiful teeth.

I sat down beside him, saying, "No, Master."

He chuckled and said, "I think you certainly have something to say, but I am enjoying the fact that you are not saying it." He looked at my giant plate of food and said, "Eat up, little one. We have work to do."

What is he talking about?

I picked up my fork and dug into the pancake on the plate which I had made for my Master. He sipped his coffee and watched me, being occasionally interrupted by different warlocks wanting to talk to him. I ate slowly, making sure to hold my head up proudly to the others in the room watching me.

The dining hall emptied out pretty quickly, but I was aware that Stephan was lingering. He eventually made his way toward us once the Master was not in conversation with anyone.

"Master, I will take Dart and show him where he will be staying," he simpered.

I gave my best *eat-shit-and-die* look to Stephan.

"No need, Stephan," Master told him. "Dart has already seen my cottage."

"But—but—"

"But what?" Master asked firmly.

Stephan recovered himself in order to say, "You don't normally have a Servant, Master."

The coven Master looked at me with a lusty smile and said, "I do now. Dart will be residing with me."

I swelled with pride at Master's words. I made a *fuck-you* face to Stephan.

"But won't you be finished with him after another day or so?" Stephan asked in shock.

"Probably not, and who are you to question me, Stephan? Get your ass out of here before I have you isolated." Master growled.

"Sorry, Master," Stephan said as he quickly stepped

backward while half-bowing. He ran into a table and I couldn't help but snigger.

"You don't like him very much, do you, little one?" Master asked me after putting a hairy arm around my shoulders. His smell immediately wafted over me, making me light-headed.

"How do you know, Master?"

"I don't know. I can just feel it."

I smiled up to him before seeing that the dining hall was empty except for Sloven and his two captains. One other older warlock came out from the bathroom and took a seat in front of us. The others followed.

"Brothers, I'm glad that you are here," Master said light-heartedly. The fact that there was a second delay and the strange translation thing happening in my head told me that they were speaking Witchspeak.

"Master, he can understand our language," Sloven said, using his head to point at me.

"I know. Dart has quite a few talents with Witchspeak being one of them," the Master informed his gang. I could hear the grunts and surprised sounds of several of the big men.

"He is a Warlock then?" the older man asked.

"I'm not sure about that," Master said carefully.

"Then how?" the older man asked. "Only Warlocks can speak our language. It is not to be understood by anyone else."

"That's true and he does have more than a little magic in him," Master said as he stared at me which caused me to blush. "But his magic seems to be centered around and including me, so I don't think he is a warlock. Anyway, we should continue to use Witchspeak so the others who are listening will not understand."

"Were you ever able to do magic before joining us, Dart?" Sloven asked me as my head translated the strange language.

"No."

"Did anything out of the ordinary happen to you that caused you to think that you were just seeing things or that you didn't really see it?" one of the others asked.

"Not that I recall," I said evenly. "But then again I was kidnapped and sold to a Russian Master who kept me as his sex slave for four years, so I think if I would have had some type of magical powers that I would have rectified that little situation."

Master smiled broadly at me.

Sloven said, "He can speak our language and smell the plants that give us power."

Master chuckled and said, "I heard that Dart was allergic to you when you rescued him, Slo."

"He was, because he could smell the hay on me," Sloven said with incredulity.

Master cut his eyes at me and said, "He is nothing if not talented . . ."

Sloven turned to my Master and asked, "He has wortcunning. What else can he do, Master?"

"Look at this," the coven Master said excitedly as he pulled the golden cigar butt out of his pocket.

Sloven took the golden object and rolled it around in his hand, carefully studying it. He handed it to the others to look at it.

"It looks like one of your cigars, Master," Sloven finally said.

"It is," the Master acknowledged. "I was holding it between my fingers when I fucked Dart after the ceremony."

"And what? It just turned into gold?"

"Yes," Master said with a chuckle. "Can you fucking believe that?"

"No, I can't," Sloven said with wide eyes. "You're saying

that when you fucked Dart that there was an alchemy spell performed?"

"Yes," the Master told him. "So, the next time, we did a little experiment and I poured water in his navel and then fucked him." My Master very dramatically reached in his pocket and produced the silver plug that had been water at one point.

"Fuck me," Sloven muttered as he took the piece of metal from his leader.

Master looked at me and I could tell he was deep in thought. "You probably should, little one."

Was he able to read my mind, because I was just thinking that I probably should fuck Sloven . . .

"Should what, Master?" It was really strange to hear my voice translated into Witchspeak.

"You probably should fuck Sloven," he stated simply.

Sloven looked up at Master and then at me before going back to the Master.

"We probably should see if his magic works with you, Slo, or if it just works with me," Master explained.

"We probably should all try it," one of the others said quickly.

Master chuckled and rubbed the back of my head. "They are all very anxious to get inside you and make magic happen, little one."

"Story of my life, Master," I said starting to laugh.

CHAPTER TEN

Part of a journal entry in the Trad Grimoud written by the Coven Master the next day, the eighth of April, two thousand nineteen.

I have had many chances to examine the Servant known as Drotik. We have banished his Russian name and are now calling him Dart. After several examinations, I have determined that Dart is worthy of my attention and I have asked him to become my Servant. He has agreed and actually believes that I might be his one true Master.

I'm not sure about that, but I do feel a draw and a connection to this marked man like no other I have ever experienced before. He told me that his real name is Gage. That is his power name and I will call him that in private.

There are many mysteries surrounding Gage and myself. We seem to be able to perform magic just by coupling our bodies. Each time I am fully embedded inside his ass, a blue ring of energy emanates from us that resulted in some very remarkable things like astral projection and life-force strengthening.

Both Gage and I are physically different when we are in proximity to each other — both of us changing for the better. The change only lasts while we are near to each other and we seem to have no control over it.

But probably the most powerful magic is done when we fuck. On two separate occasions now, Gage and I have fucked where we both have reached our release. On the first occasion, I was holding a cigar which turned into solid gold as I held it. The second occasion, I poured water into Gage's belly button which turned to sil-

ver at the end of the fuck.

Gage and I are meeting with the senior leadership of the gang today to report these findings and answer any questions that we are able to address. Hopefully, they might have some insight on why this is happening and what is the reason.

"You want me to fuck him to see what will happen?" Sloven asked.

"Yes. It is worthy of an experiment," Master said firmly.

Sloven cut his eyes at me. "I guess we could do that some-time this afternoon."

"You will do it now. And you will do it right here on top of this table," Master demanded.

"In front of you, Master?"

"Yes," my Master answered. "I will see for myself what his power is."

"Yes, Master," Sloven said with a strange mixture of ac-ceptance and excitement.

"Up onto the table, Dart," Master ordered me. He picked up a ladybug that had been crawling across the table and held it between his hands. He bowed and opened his hands onto the table. A very soft-looking blanket suddenly appeared.

I backed up to the table and lay back on the blanket. Mas-ter helped me slide a little further back as I watched Sloven getting undressed.

Nothing compared to the lust I felt for my Master, but Sloven would have been a close second. I was so totally turned on by his blond military haircut that it was hard not to look at his enormous biceps, covered in dark tattoos, and his beautiful chest. But my eyes were drawn away when he dropped his jeans and I saw his long fat dick.

"Does every warlock come packing, Master?" I asked flippantly. My cock was once again as hard as a rock.

"Just the ones that will satisfy your hungry hole, little one," he answered immediately. The others laughed in the background. "Would you like to stuff something in his mouth to keep him quiet, Slo?"

"No, I'm ready to go," he said.

Sloven climbed onto the table and straddled me. I lifted my legs onto his broad shoulders and he promptly bent me in half. I was grateful that the table was sturdy and well-made.

"Jaxon, can you produce some lube?" Master asked.

I watched as one of the other wizards reached into a glass of water left on the table and put his hands together. "Sure thing, Master."

The coven Master produced a fat cigar between his palms and handed it to Sloven. The man above me clenched it between his teeth and lit it with a wave of his hand. He took a couple of puffs on the cigar and then blew the smoke into my face while I lubed his big cock.

"Ready, Dart?"

"Let the experiment begin," I said, tongue-in-cheek.

Sloven began by slowing pushing his big dick inside me, almost like he was afraid of what was going to happen.

"So tight," he said between his clenched teeth.

"I told you," Master said. His dark eyes were intently studying my face while I was being fucked. He looked like he was seriously worried about something happening, also.

When Sloven hit the end of his fuck stick and was fully embedded inside me, he let out a soft moan.

Master said, "Well, there is no blue energy ring with the two of you." He had a look of extreme relief on his face now. "Fuck him," Master commanded, whether it was meant for me or Sloven, I wasn't sure.

Sloven tented himself over me, holding himself up with his dark tatted arms and slowly pulled back and thrust inside me again. He did this a couple of times while I held onto either his thick neck or his ripped biceps.

"Fuck him hard, Slo," Master growled. "He won't break. Trust me, I've already tried to fucking destroy him."

Sloven picked up the pace and was soon giving me a good hard fuck. We were both sweating in the closed space and my balls signaled to me that they were ready to empty about the same time that I felt the big warlock's cock pulse inside me for the same reason.

"I'm going to cum, Master," I said with my eyes closed.

"Me, too," Sloven announced breathlessly.

"Do it," Master encouraged us.

My cum vent opened a few seconds ahead of Sloven's, so I pumped my hot load directly onto my stomach and chest.

"Fuccccckkkkkkk!" Sloven growled around his cigar as he felt my tightened ass muscles strangling his cock. He lost his shit and pumped his magical elixir deep inside my ass.

"That's good," Master said. He stepped over and reached for Sloven's cigar. "Let's see what happened."

The coven Master held up the cigar for us all to see and it was a shiny silver color. My Master's face looked disappointed.

"It turned to silver," the older wizard said.

"No," Master said instantly. "It's not heavy." He took his fingernail and pressed it into the cigar. It opened a hole in the surface and I could see brown tobacco underneath. "It's aluminum," he finally said.

"What the fuck?" Sloven asked, having finally regained himself. I made a quick mental note that he wasn't moving off of me and his dick was still hard and pulsing inside of me.

"I might have an explanation, Master," I said quietly.

He looked at me like he had just caught me cheating on him. Finally, he said, "Go ahead, little one."

"I think a lot of the elements were here that produces our magic, Master."

"Explain," he ordered.

"Well, I was getting fucked hard by a big cock, I hit my release, but more importantly, you were right next to me. I could see your handsome face, my nose was full of your smell, and I could feel your emotions."

"So?"

"So, I think that was enough to produce a spark of magic and turn the shell of the cigar to the thinnest of metals."

He nodded his head and said, "It's an interesting theory, Dart. It will require another test."

"Yes, Master," I said, having already realized that another test would be forthcoming.

"Jaxon, you will fuck Dart next," Master commanded.

"Yes, Master," the big warlock said quickly. His hungry eyes were all over me.

I hadn't really given him much of a thought before, but I checked him out now. He looked like he was around thirty-five years old with brown hair shaved short against his skull. He looked more like a member of a motorcycle gang than any of the others in the room. Jaxon's biceps were covered with tattoos which looked great against his black tank top. Jeans and black biker boots finished his look.

"I'll move over here," Master said as he went two tables away.

I could still feel his presence even from there. "I'm not sure that is going to do it, Master."

"Why not, little one?"

"I think you have to go further, Master."

"How far?"

"Until we change, Master," I told him. I saw the dawning of realization cross his face.

"You are very smart, little one," he said as he handed Jaxon a new cigar. "But you know that I will have to punish you later for all this talking that you are doing here, don't you?"

"Yes, Master." The idea of my big Master punishing me filled me with both excitement and dread. I was torn between wanting the punishment and trying to avoid it.

"Can he come again so soon, Master?" Jaxon asked the coven Master, who was walking to the far side of the dining hall from us.

"He can when I fuck him, Jaxon."

I waited for the change in my body, but it didn't come even when Master got to the far wall and turned around to face us. "We have to get further away," I said as I slid off the table and moved to one against the wall.

Suddenly a shudder ran through my body and it felt like someone had poked a hole in the inflatable muscle suit that I was wearing.

"Holy Mother," the older warlock whispered. He was staring at me with wide eyes.

I looked across the room at my Master and saw his glorious long hair first. He had changed just like I had. We were far enough apart now. I lay down on the table and lifted my legs.

Jaxon was a good fuck, but I had to jack my own cock in order to reach my release. He came first, but kept his cock in me until I joined him in squirting my load. He complimented me on the tightness of my hole and how much he enjoyed fucking me constantly throughout the exercise.

"Well?" My Master's deep voiced boomed from across the room. He had started to walk toward us now that the fuck was over and I felt my body puff up as he got close.

Jaxon held up the cigar to Sloven who examined it.

"No change," Sloven answered.

"As we suspected," Master said. He reached down and

put his oversized hand on the side of my face. He gently ran his rough thumb across my lips as he looked down at me with desire. "I hope you are satisfied now that Dart is not a warlock, but is some kind of conduit for my magical powers."

A conduit? *That was very smart of Master. I didn't even considered that possibility.*

Master helped me into a seated position and I winced from the pain that immediately shot up my spinal cord from my sore ass.

Sloven looked a little sheepish as he asked, "Master, may we have one more experiment?"

The others turned to him with surprised looks and Master asked, "What else would you like to see, Slo?"

"I would like to experience the blue energy ring and also see the transmutation in person if the Master does not mind," he said carefully.

"You don't believe me?" Master's voice boomed in the closed hall.

"I believe you, Master. I just think there might be something we could learn by observing the process."

"You definitely will learn how my Servant likes to be fucked by observing the process," Master said with a laugh. "But I see your point." He looked down at me and asked, "Can you go again, Dart?"

"Always for you, Master."

"Good answer. Marco, can you produce some leather straps for me? Rubio, will you get two pieces of charcoal from the fire pit for me. Jaxon, I need a piece of paper. Sloven, I need a ball gag from my cottage."

I watched in fascination as each wizard began to conjure the items that the Master asked for. The two wizards that had to leave to get the specific items that he asked for did not take long and they were soon back.

"The others are very curious about what is happening

here," Sloven told his Master in a calm voice.

"They will especially want to know after the blue energy beam shoots out of here in a minute," Master told him.

"By the way, what has happened to the plants in your cottage? Did you perform a fast growth spell?"

"It's the result of the blue energy," Master told him with a wink.

"Really?" Sloven asked.

I debated about whether to say anything or not because of the punishment that Master had promised me, but I couldn't help myself. "The blue ring seems to grant one or the other of us something that we desire."

Sloven looked at me like I was crazy.

So, I continued, "The first time we fucked, I wanted to see my father more than anything and he appeared in the blue energy and we got to speak."

Master continued the story by saying, "The second time, I wanted the nargelia plant I was growing to bloom so that I could use it in a potion that I was creating, and the energy ring affected my plants. Even my dried herbs came back to life."

"The third time, Master was fucking me in a dark room and I desperately wanted to watch him as he destroyed my ass, so the blue ring became a map of the heavens on the ceiling that allowed just enough light for me to see my Master in action."

"What the fuck do you think it is, Master?"

"I don't know, Slo, but it seems to be positive for us. I think it is an elemental."

"So, it's not bane?"

Master looked down at me and said, "That means *evil* or *bad*."

"I don't think so."

"There's no way that it could be evil when the most fantastic thing that has ever happened to me causes it to appear," I said defensively.

"The most fantastic?" Master asked with a raised eyebrow.

I blushed immediately and nodded my head.

He tousled my hair and said, "I feel the same way, little one. Now, let's put on a fucking show for these boys."

"Yes, sir!"

CHAPTER ELEVEN

Part of a police report filed by detectives outside Charleston, South Carolina on the eighth of April, 2019.

Mr. Frank Howard appeared in the station yesterday to file another missing person's report. We are all very aware of the case. Mr. Howard had a son, Gage, who happened to become marked on his thirteenth birthday. He went missing on his way home from school four years ago at the age of fourteen.

Our detectives are sure that the boy was taken. Reports of other marked boys from other cities confirm that there was a gang of kidnappers working in the south during that year. We traced a transaction between the gang and an Eastern European Mafia family. From there the trail has gone cold.

Mr. Howard has kept in touch with us every year on the anniversary of the kidnapping. He has never had any information to offer us until this time, so we took note. Mr. Howard reports that he was contacted by his son two days ago, but when we questioned him about it, he became embarrassed.

Mr. Howard reports that his son came to him as a blue vision. He had fallen asleep on the couch in front of the TV and was awakened by a crackling sound. When he adjusted his eyes, he saw a blue swirling smoke which after a few seconds materialized into a figure. He swears that it was his son, so he called out to him.

The blue smoke figure answered his father, telling him that he was okay and had been rescued from his kidnappers. Before he could ask anything else, there was some shouting and the smoky figure disappeared.

Clearly Mr. Howard is experiencing visual hallucinations based on his unresolved grief. His report does not seem credible, but he is one hundred percent convinced that the figure he saw in the swirling blue smoke was Gage. We have assured Mr. Howard that we will alert him as soon as we hear anything from Europe or from home.

Master and I were still in the dining room with the senior leadership of the gang. We had already performed several experiments to test any magical power that I might have had, which led to me being fucked hard twice. But I was just about to get the hardest hammer of all because the wizards had asked their coven Master to fuck me one more time.

My new Master had asked the members of his gang to gather some unusual materials and I was dying to ask him what they were going to be used for. But I knew better. I could feel the lust rolling off of him and my desire to please him was just as strong as his lust.

With a wave of his hand, he lowered one of the tables and commanded, "Up on the table, Dart." He waved his hand at the previous table I had used and the blanket flew through the air onto the new table.

I quickly moved to the table and put my back down onto it.

"On all fours, little one. I want you hanging from my cock like a sausage drying on a hook."

I stared at him, slack-jawed as he put several kitchen towels down on the table for me. The things that Master said to me made me feel things that I had never felt before. He was unlike any man I had ever met.

"Now!" he snapped, bringing me back to reality.

I scrambled to obey him.

Once I was on the table on all fours, he announced, "If my Servant and I do this, then whatever we make here shall be used to fund a trip to the States for Dart to go see his father.

Agreed?"

"Agreed, Master," the men said in unison.

I was super happy that my Master was going to keep his word and let me see my father. It made me want to please him even more than I already did.

"Excellent. Put your wrists beside each other in the small of your back, Dart."

I had to kneel to do this without falling but followed his order, and he promptly tied my wrists together with a piece of leather. He put an item into each of my palms, one was charcoal and the other was charcoal wrapped in a piece of paper based on the feel of them.

"Do you need lubed, little one?" he asked jerking the leather straps tied to my arms.

"No, Master, but may I make your cock slick with my saliva before you put my gag on?"

He chuckled and said, "You are a smart cookie, Dart, and yes, you may."

Master held my chin up with one hand as he fed his massive hummer inside my mouth. I sucked on it as much as I could from this position, trying to get it as wet as possible. I loved the taste of his cock and he had to pull it out of my still-sucking mouth before he blew a load right down my throat.

"Very nice, Dart, but not part of the experiment," he said chuckling as he stretched the ball gag over my head and fit it into my mouth. "Now, be quiet so I can ride this sweet ass of yours."

I could hear the other warlocks whispering, and I knew that they were talking about how I would ever be able to take Master's huge cock. They were about to see . . .

Master placed one huge hand on my stomach and held my hip steady with the other one while he pushed his cock head through my anal ring. My ass squeezed him tight as he broke through my barrier and began to plow a hot furrow through my ass.

"Fuck! You are so tight for me, little one."

Always, Master.

Master kept pushing and pushing until he was finally buried completely to the nuts inside me. As soon as I felt his short hairs tickling my ass cheeks, I saw the blue ring of energy that had emanated from us. I realized that my knees were off of the table and that I was suspended completely from Master's cock.

I heard the shock of the wizards and saw them trying to touch the blue energy. It hovered for a couple of seconds, letting the wizards examine it, but then it continued across the dining hall and through the walls.

Once the blue energy was gone, Master got down to fucking. He moved his hand from my stomach to my throat, swinging me back and forth along his substantial shaft. It took my breath away. I mean each of the fucks that Master had given me up until this point had been fantastic, but there was no comparison to this one. It was amazing.

Master fucked me faster, harder, and deeper than before and when he let go of my throat and just used the leather reins from my tied wrists, I thought I might lose my shit right there from the very visual of it in my head. Master was a dominant who knew how to make me feel completely like he was in charge and that I belonged to him in every way, and I couldn't have been happier about it.

I felt totally exhausted by the time that Master and I came within seconds of each other. He roared with his release as he flooded my dark chamber from deep inside and I moaned against the gag in my mouth as my cock shot strand after strand of hot spunk all over the table.

As I regained myself, I realized that someone was pounding on the door. Sloven had redressed and now he went to see who it was. Master reached down and undid my gag.

"That was exceptional, Gage," he whispered to me. "We might have to do that again soon."

"Yes, Master," I agreed.

Sloven came striding back to the table with a huge grin on his face.

"What?" Master asked.

He asked, "Did you need anything in particular when the blue energy ring came, Master?"

"Not that I can think of. I only needed Dart's fine asshole squeezing my cock."

I looked up and back at him sheepishly.

"Did you need something, Dart?" he asked.

"Sorry, Master. I wasn't thinking about it."

"But you were thinking about something," he stipulated.

"I was thinking that I needed a hot bath, Master," I admitted.

Master turned to his number two and asked, "What is it?"

Sloven looked like he was the cat who had swallowed the canary. "Apparently the blue energy left the dining hall and centered around your cottage, Master. When the smoke cleared, some of the gang discovered that you have a brand new hot tub behind your cottage."

Master looked down at me and a grin spread over his handsome face. "That could be fun. Let us see what else our experiment has produced."

I felt the slack come with sweet relief as my Master untied my hands. I pulled my arms forward just as Master grabbed my wrists and rubbed them between his hot palms. I was very aware that Master was still planted deep inside me and that he was still rock hard.

"Open your right hand, Dart," Master commanded.

I slowly opened my fingers and resting there in my palm was a charcoal briquette shaped diamond. It was fucking huge and heavy as shit. I had never seen anything that sparkled the way it did.

"Fuck me," Sloven said in almost a whisper.

"Is that a real diamond?" the older wizard asked.

Master reached into my hand and picked up the diamond. He waved his hand over the table and a clear sheet of glass was soon covering it. The coven Master touched the diamond to the glass, pressed down, and moved it across the pane of glass. "It cuts glass," he said.

"And the other one, Master?" Jaxon asked greedily.

"Open your left hand, little one," Master ordered. His cock throbbed like a heartbeat inside my ass.

Slowly, I opened my fingers and saw that the paper was now an orange color.

Master picked up the object in my hand and laughed out loud. "Look at this," he said as he held the object in front of my eyes. The paper had turned to copper and inside the copper tube was another fucking big-ass diamond.

Master held the piece of art up so that the other wizards could see it. They made all kind of noises as they passed the unusual object around and marveled at it.

"Well done, Dart."

"You as well, Master. I can feel that you are not finished here."

"Oh, I'm going to fucking rail you out one more time, Dart, don't you worry, but I just wanted to make sure that we had answered all of these boys' questions first before I do."

"I think we are good," Sloven said as he visually checked with each of the senior leaders.

"Go enjoy the hot tub while I enjoy this hot hole of Dart's," Master told his fellow warlocks.

"Thanks," they muttered as they left the dining hall, some of them obviously disappointed that there were no more experiments which would enable them to fuck me.

We were soon alone and my Master lifted me by the throat until my back was pressed against his hairy chest. He held me there with one hand on my throat and the other wandering all over my body.

"I will let you go soak in the hot tub after this, Gage. I just want to show you how happy I am with you for today."

"Show me, Master. Show me hard," I moaned as he tweaked my nipples and pulled on my hardening cock.

My Master's hips started to pull his big cock out of my ass and then methodically push it back inside. He kept my anal ring spread to its limits and punched my prostate over and over again with each thrust. "You are the most exciting thing that has ever happened to me, my Servant. I can't seem to be able to get enough of you."

"I feel the same way, Master. I am consumed by you." I rode the waves that his thighs and crotch made as his hips worked that massive meat inside me like I was in a raft on the high seas.

"Tomorrow night is the black moon, Gage. You and I will do marvelous magic during it and then we will depart to go see your father. It is my promise to you."

"I am grateful to you, my Master."

"You should be, my Servant."

"I am yours to do with what you want."

"And what I want is to be doing this to you for a very long time in the future. I will make sure you are safe and happy and we will be made rich from our fucking. And you will be mine, always."

His hot hand on my throat was so fucking sexy that I felt my insides start to bloom with desire. My cock was as hard as it possibly could get and my balls were hanging lower than ever.

"Always, Master." His words were having some kind of effect on me, putting me into some kind of dream state where nothing existed but his cock and my ass. His smell was in my nose and his chest hair was scratching my back, all of which was overstimulating me.

"You are an amazing man, Gage," Master said in-between hard thrusts into the deepest darkest parts of my ass.

"I am but a reflection of who you want me to be, Master."

Both of our breathings were becoming labored now and sweat was pouring off of us onto the dining hall table.

"We are one, you and I," he said. "It is both of us together that makes the magic."

"But you have always known that, Master."

"Yes, but I've never had a connection like the one that I have with you."

"Me either, true Master."

"And the magic has never flowed like this before with anyone. It is like the two of us are bigger than the laws of nature that has governed us for the last millennium."

I moaned with a ragged voice, "I know you're cock is bigger than any that I have seen in nature before and that is all that I am aware of at the present moment, Master."

"And your ass is its Master," he said, his voice equally harsh and rough with desire.

"Make my ass yours, Master," I said as I pumped up and down on his big stick like a merry-go-round horse.

"It is already mine," he said hoarsely.

"Show it, Master," I commanded. My hand dropped down to grasp my cock just as it exploded with my orgasm.

Master was three seconds behind me. He pushed me forward with a firm hand on the middle of my back. I caught myself by bracing the table with my free hand. I lowered my face down to the smooth tabletop and felt Master's eruption just as it happened.

He filled me with his seed, but then without warning, my Master pulled his big spurting cock out of my ass and shot his wad directly onto my ass and lower back. It was a hot way to make my ass his own and I couldn't help but smile to myself, despite the fact that my ass felt empty and my asshole was quivering to be stretched out again.

Suddenly a strange burning sensation began on the small of my back and ran down to the top of my ass. At first I thought it was just my Master's cum that was super-heating my skin, but then I knew it was something else. The heat was too hot and there was a slight smell in the air of burning flesh.

I raised and twisted my head to look back. Master was motionless with his eyes closed and his hand wrapped around his still dribbling dick. As if he felt my eyes on him, he opened his and looked at me.

Then he looked at my ass. "Gage," he said softly.

"Master, what is happening?" The pain was starting to subside now, but it still hurt like hell.

"I have marked you as mine, little one."

"Literally?"

"Yes. Would you like to see?"

"Yes, Master."

Master picked up a stray piece of silverware off one of the tables and held it between his palms. He lowered his head and I saw his lips moving, causing his unshaven face to make subtle movements.

He opened his hands and produced a mirror the size of his enormous paw. He held it up and calculated the angle between my eyes and the top of my ass. After a few adjustments, he finally had it.

I saw in the mirror that a very dark mark like a tattoo was now emblazoned upon my skin. Half of it covered my lower back and the other half covered the top of my ass. It was gloriously intricate and beautifully rendered, even though I couldn't tell what it was a picture of.

"Do you like it, Gage?"

"Very much, Master. I would like anything that marks me as yours."

"Do you know what it is, little one?"

"No, Master."

"It's a honeysuckle bush in bloom."

"It is your sign, Master."

"Yes."

"Is it a tattoo, Master?"

"No," he said as he ran his hand over the mark on my ass and lower back. "It is called a claiming and it is very old magic. It is a psychic mark placed on something that is desired."

"You placed it there, Master?"

"No. Our magic put it there, little one. I did not do the spell."

"You might as well have, Master," I said happily as I sighed contentedly.

CHAPTER TWELVE

Part of a journal entry in the Trad Grimoud written by the Coven Master the next day, the ninth of April, 2019.

I have made the marked man known as Drotik my Servant. I call him by his real name, Gage, when we are alone. The gang calls him Dart.

Gage and I are connected on multiple levels. When we are far apart from each other, we experience physical discomfort. When we are in close physical proximity to each other, we actually physically change to a better version of ourselves or a version that the other one likes better. It is the most amazing spell that I have ever encountered.

Every time that Gage and I fuck, at the first moment that I am buried up to the hilt inside his sweet ass, some type of energy is released. It is blue in color and smoky in shape. This blue energy seems to be some kind of heart's desire spell. Each time we have produced the blue energy something that one of us has desired has happened or appeared.

In addition, each time that Gage and I fuck, we both cum within seconds of each other. If either of us are touching a plant or an object made from plants during the fuck, then it turns into a precious metal. We turn carbon into diamonds with just the power of our fucking.

The senior leaders of the gang gathered and we performed several experiments with Gage's help and found all of these things to be consistent and reliable. Gage and I even fucked afterward and unwittingly turned a kitchen towel that we were kneeling on into a sheet of pure bronze.

Gage would like to go to America to visit his father and I have promised him that I would accompany him. Tonight is the black moon and we will both be present and participate and then we will leave for the United States. I have not yet told Gage what the plans are for tonight, but he will find out soon enough.

Master was true to his word. He let me soak for several hours in the hot tub as he conducted gang business. I was joined off and on by several of the warlocks who wanted to try out the new spa. They were all handsome studs in their primes whom I would normally be all over, but now that I had met my true Master, there was no one for me but him.

Late in the afternoon, I opened my eyes and was surprised to see some of the marked men standing around the hot tub.

"Hi, guys," I greeted them.

"Hi, Dart," they returned in English.

"Mind if we join you?" one known as Cobo asked.

"No, jump in," I said. "I'm all shriveled up, anyway."

"We want you to stay," a handsome teenager named Vesely said. "We haven't had a chance to get to know you yet."

I noticed that none of my Russian friends were here, but neither was the ass, Stephan, so I was inclined to stay. "Okay, but I'm going to sit on the edge so that you guys have more room."

The six men laughed as they crawled into the hot water and settled into the seats. They all introduced themselves to me.

"This feels so good," the one called Tripod said. It was easy to see how he had earned his nickname since the men were totally naked.

"Especially after entertaining Sloven all afternoon, huh, Pod?" Vesely asked. I could see the glaze of ambition in his eyes from my spot on the side of the spa.

"His dick is so fucking big," Tripod groaned. "It feels like my ass is never going to recover."

"Not as big as the Master's," Vesely said with wide eyes as he looked at me. "I heard you got fucked by Sloven, Jaxon, and the Master this morning in the dining hall," he said with such reverence that I thought he might have been in church if I didn't know better.

"Vesely!" Tor said sharply. "That was told to you in secret."

Vesely arched his back and said, "What? Dart probably doesn't care. He is probably proud of it."

All of the marked men turned toward me. "I wouldn't say that I was proud, but I also have nothing to hide," I said evenly with a shrug.

"So, it's true, Dart?" Tor asked.

"I have been blessed to catch the eye of the Master," I answered him without really answering.

"I don't think it is his eye that you caught, Dart," a Servant named Pieta said.

This made everyone laugh really hard.

"I am fortunate."

"Can you take him all, Dart? I hear he is huge," Vesely said almost in a whisper.

"He hasn't complained," I said, deftly avoiding the question.

"We just thought the Master would never favor anyone," Tor said. "I mean, until you appeared, he really never gave us much thought."

"But he fucked around with you, didn't he?"

"He picks one of us for the black moon spell, but usually that is it. He took Torsch back to his cottage one night after the black moon, which was unusual for him, but the Master has not asked for him since."

I thought that was strange, now knowing how much sex Master liked to have. I would have to ask him how he has survived without using the gang's Servants.

Pieta asked, "Has he told you what you will do tonight, Dart?"

"No. Just that we will make powerful magic." As soon as the phrase was out of my mouth, I felt my muscles puff up with energy.

"And that we will." My Master's booming voice sounded behind me.

"Master," I said huskily as I realized that he was close.

I turned just as he sidled up beside me on the side of the hot tub.

He immediately draped his arm over my shoulders. Master looked into the hot tub and said, "This looks like a marked man soup. Is that what we are having for dinner?"

I laughed, but the others just stared at him slack-jawed.

"You may join us, Master, if you wish," Vesely said, recovering faster than the others.

I narrowed my eyes at the man who was trying so hard to steal my man.

"I can do anything that I wish, Vesely. I don't need your permission," Master snapped.

"Of course not, Master," he said, bowing his head.

I smiled at Master's admonishment of the head-strong Servant. Master looked down at me and I saw curiosity cross his face as he looked at mine. *Was he wondering why I am smiling? Can he tell that I am fearful that I will lose him?* I hoped not.

Master looked back and forth between me and the men in the hot tub for a few seconds. Then it was his turn to smile. His hand dropped from my shoulder to my hip and ass cheek. He turned back to the men in the spa and said, "But I am glad that you are here, Vesely. You will come to my cottage in a half hour."

Vesely looked up with such joy on his face that I wanted to slap it right off of him. "Yes, Master. Of course, Master. I'll be there, Master."

"Ugh," I said softly, causing Master to give me a stare.

"In the cottage, Dart," he ordered.

I didn't know if he was mad at me or not, but I didn't want to make it worse by not following his commands fast enough. I scrambled out of the hot tub and grabbed my towel.

"Did you get a tattoo, Dart?" the closest Servant to me asked after I had turned around.

I could feel all of their eyes on me now.

"The Master marked me as his own," I said simply, turning so that they could get a better look at my back and butt.

Vesely's eyes widened and he addressed my Master. "That's your mark, Master," he said in disbelief. "You claimed him, Master?"

"I do not have to explain myself to you, Vesely," the coven Master snapped. "But, yes, I have claimed Dart as mine."

"But a claiming is permanent," Tor said in astonishment.

"What's your point?" the Master asked him.

"Nothing . . . Master. Uh, congratulations, Master," he said, stumbling over his words.

"Dart, do you belong to me?" Master asked me directly.

"Yes, Master."

"Did you want me to mark you as my own?"

"I did, Master."

"Do you want to be with me forever?"

"Yes, Master."

My Master looked at the Servants in the hot tub and said, "Well, there it is. There is no issue." He snapped his fingers and pointed at the cottage.

I lowered my head and walked quickly into the cottage

that I shared with my Master. I was overjoyed and suddenly dreading that the sounds of his footsteps followed me inside.

"Lay on the bed on your stomach, Gage," he commanded.

Oh, good. I'm just going to get fucked instead of receiving a lecture . . .

I followed his orders while I watched him searching for things in a drawer and then in his closet. He came back to the bed with several leather straps and a bar gag. I was sure that my eyes had widened as my face lay on the top of the mattress.

"I believe that it is time for your punishment, Gage."

I could tell from his voice that this was turning him on just as much as fucking me. I didn't need to see his hard cock to tell me that.

"Tell me why I have to punish you, little one."

"I-I . . ."

"Spit it out, Gage." He growled.

"I spoke when I was not asked a question, Master."

"Yes, and?"

"I did not defer to you when we were experimenting, Master," I guessed, having trouble really remembering what my other infractions were.

"Yes." He began to pull my arms back and bound my wrists in the small of my back. "You will respect me as your Master, Gage."

I do, Master . . .

He also bound my ankles together. "You will obey me, Gage."

Is he mad at me? Yes, Master . . .

"You will do all the things that I want you to do. You will be the ultimate showpiece for me—a reflection of me in every way. I will depend upon you for this, Gage. You will not disappoint me."

I will not disappoint you, Master . . .

He easily lifted me from my prone position and placed

me onto the rug at the end of the bed. "I want you to kneel, little one," he said softly.

I bent my legs back so that he could deposit me on my knees onto the rug. It took me a few seconds to get my balance, but fortunately my Master held me steady until I did.

Once I was able to kneel without assistance, he backed away from me and said, "Almost complete." He turned back to the bed and grabbed the bar gag that he had placed there.

Stepping toward me with it, I got a good look at the gag. It was a straight piece of rubber tubing with a metal bar running through the middle of it. Metal brackets on either end held it up and leather straps ran out from them. It was pretty simple but pretty ingenious.

"I did not like the sound that you made when I showed favoritism to one of the marked men, Gage. In fact, I didn't like that you made a sound at all. My decisions are not to be questioned. My decisions should not and will not be run through you first. If I want your opinion about anything that I am doing, I will ask for it. Do you understand?"

"Yes, Master," I said, lowering my head in shame.

He immediately put two fingers under my chin and lifted my head until my green eyes were looking at his dark eyes. "Do not beat yourself up, little one. You are still learning how to serve me best and I am not entirely used to being a Master yet. Well, I am used to being the Master of the warlocks, but I am new to having a Servant all to myself."

That made me feel better, but all that did was leave space in my mind for other things. Master needed to hurry if we were going to fuck because Vesely would be here any minute to interrupt us.

Master slowly fit the rubber tubing between my teeth and carefully fit the gag onto my face. The braces went over my ears and toward the back of my head where he laced the straps securely.

He stepped back, admiring his work. "Nice, very nice, Gage. You look magnificent."

I didn't try to respond.

Suddenly there was a knock on the door and I panicked a little that Vesely would see me in this position of submission. Master did not miss my reaction.

"Vesely is here," Master said. "You will stay silent and watch. If you close your eyes, I will force them open and put something there to hold them open. You will not look down. You will watch everything. Do you understand?"

I nodded. This was going to be extremely difficult because one, I didn't want my Master to fuck Vesely and two, I didn't want Vesely to have the pleasure of seeing me in this subservient position while he got my Master's attention.

"If you look away or make a noise, I will extend your punishment twice as long. Do you understand, my Servant?"

I nodded, realizing that there was no way out of this. I would have to take my punishment and make him proud of me.

"Very good," he said as he waved his hand at the door, opening it.

"Master?" Vesely's weasel-sounding voice asked from the doorway.

"Come here," Master commanded.

My cock hardened instantly at Master's command, even though it wasn't directed to me.

Vesely walked forward quickly.

"Born in a barn?" Master grumbled under his breath as he waved his hand and closed the door.

"Pardon me, Master?"

"Shut up, Vesely. I don't want you to talk anymore."

"Yes," he began, before nodding his head instead. His gaze flicked over to me and I saw his eyes widen.

"Get on your knees, bitch. I need to be satisfied." Master growled.

Vesely snapped his head back toward the Master and then quickly dropped down onto his knees. Master stripped off his jeans and sat down on the end of the bed, sporting a huge hard-on.

I realized at once that Master and I were close enough so that we were still in our perfected physical states. That meant that Master's dong was at an unbelievable size. I smiled around my gag as I mentally challenged Vesely to take that big piece of meat.

The Servant moved forward and grasped Master's cock by the base. I couldn't see his face, but I could only imagine that Vesely was trying hard to figure out what he was going to be able to do with it. His head was soon bobbing up and down on Master's cock, but I could see from the depth of his bobs that he was not getting very much of Master's meat into his mouth each time.

This was confirmed when Master put his hand on the back of Vesely's head and tried desperately to push it further down on his hard rod. Vesely gagged and choked.

"God dammit!" Master shouted as he finally just pulled Vesely off of his cock. "It's like having a dog slobbering on me. Hopefully your ass is going to be better than that face hole of yours."

I didn't miss that Master shot me a quick look as he was voicing his disappointment with Vesely. That one furtive glance made me happier than ever.

"Are you lubed?" Master asked.

"I can be in a minute, Master."

"Why the fuck aren't you prepared, Vesely? Where did you think you were going? To a goddamn tea party?"

"Sorry, Master. I didn't know. I'll be ready in a quick minute," he said as he scrambled to the bathroom.

"You have nothing to fear, little one," he said huskily as he stared at me. "This one is all talk and ambition and no talent."

Vesely was back, his ass shiny from the lube.

"Sit on it since you can't swallow it," Master commanded.

Vesely tried and tried, but was never able to get more than the head and a few inches of shaft past his anal ring before giving up. He was in so much pain that the tears fell silently down his face.

I felt sorry for him even as we stared at each other, as he tried over and over to relax enough to take my Master's cock.

Master finally gave up and said, "On the bed on all fours, Vesely. I'm going to give you one more chance."

Vesely popped off of his cock, looking very grateful to be free. He put his head down and assumed the position on the bed.

The coven Master was able to get a little more purchase this time around, but it was wholly unsuccessful. I could feel the smile on my face despite my best attempts to remove it.

Finally, the big warlock smacked Vesely on the back and said, "It's just not going to work, Vesely." He pulled his hard pole out of the Servant's ass. "Let me show you how to get your Master's attention."

I was just trying to process that comment when I realized that Master was coming toward me. It was thrilling to realize that he was going to fuck me and to do it right in front of Vesely was icing on the cake.

Master sat down on the floor behind me. Removing my ankle restraints, he lifted my hips like I weighed nothing and lowered me down onto his lap. I kept my lower legs bent back on either side of his hips. My Master pushed my back forward and slipped the head of his massive hummer into my ass.

I closed my eyes and tried to relax as Master pulled me down onto his long prong. His cock filled me up like none other each and every time. I moaned out loud around the bar gag as I reached the base of his cock and realized that he was completely buried inside me.

Master pulled me back until my back rested against his strong chest. "Feet up on my thighs, little one," he commanded.

I followed his order and watched as he spread his legs, opening mine at the same time. It occurred to me that he was showing Vesely all of us and I couldn't have been prouder.

"That is how you get your Master's attention," the coven Master said with a husky tone behind me just as the blue smoke appeared.

Chapter Thirteen

Part of a letter from Gage, Servant to the coven Master of the Warlock Motorcycle Gang of Romania to his father in the United States written the morning of the tenth of April, 2019.

Hi Dad,

It's been so long that I know this must come as a shock. I don't know whether you actually were aware of me when we talked the other night or not, so this letter might give you a heart attack. I certainly hope not.

I am fine and have been freed from my imprisonment. I have found my true Master, and he has promised me that we will come to visit you next week. I have so much to tell you, but at the same time, I don't know where to start. I don't know how much you want to know or how much I should tell you. I don't want to hurt you anymore than you have already been.

I am anxious to catch up with you and assure you that you did nothing wrong. I have spent four years worrying that you have blamed yourself for my abduction. There was nothing you could have done, Dad. It was my own foolish mistake or teenage horniness that led to my capture. I had no one to blame except for myself and the people who captured me.

I can't wait to see you and hear all the news from the time that I have missed. Rationally, I feel like I should be bitter or mentally ill at this point, but I am actually in a very good place. Unbelievably, I was rescued by a group of men who have asked me to join their ranks. Their leader is the man who I believe is my true Master. He is the most amazing man that I have ever met, and I cannot wait for you to meet him. I hope that you will like him as much as I do.

Don't worry about picking me up at the airport or anything. I'm not sure how I will be able to enter the country without any paperwork, but I have complete faith in my Master to find a way.

"What is the black moon, Master?" I asked. Master and I had just finished dinner and had come back to our cottage to get some sleep so that we would be rested for tonight's activities. But of course, once we were in bed, we had to fuck.

We were spooned into each other—my back against his broad hairy chest and his cock was firmly planted inside my ass even though he had just pumped another huge load of hot man cream into my guts. I loved feeling the heat of his skin on mine and the way his rough hands roamed over my body absentmindedly drove me to another hard-on immediately.

"It is a time of high magic, little one," Master answered. "It is when our powers are amplified and we can do really special things."

I chuckled and said, "I'm not sure our powers need to be amplified, Master."

"You could be right, Gage. I'm looking forward to seeing what will happen with you underneath me tonight."

"Will it be dark magic, Master?" I asked softly.

"The black moon amplifies any magic. We do not conjure demons or cast spells on others for evil reasons. Our gang is dedicated to making wrongs right like we did when we rescued you, Gage."

"Did you know what you were rescuing, Master?"

He laughed behind me, making the hair on the back of my head move with his breath. "I didn't even know what you were once you were here, little one. How could I have known?"

"And now, Master?"

"I still don't know, but I think you might be an angel."

Now it was my turn to laugh. "Trust me, I am no angel."

"The way you work that ass and mouth on my cock has to be a skill that is heaven-sent," Master said with a husky voice. "What other explanation could it be?"

"I'm glad that you think so, Master. I will continue to try to keep your interest."

"You are mine. Have you forgotten the mark I placed on you?" He ran one of his fingertips over the honeysuckle mark on my lower back. "I will not be losing interest in you anytime soon."

"I have not forgotten, Master. I am yours and you may do with me what you wish."

"Damn straight." He growled. "Now, I wish for us both to get some sleep so that we are fresh tonight."

"Can we fuck when we wake, Master?"

"No, but you can blow me if you desire."

"Thank you, Master," I said sleepily as I closed my eyes. I was safe and warm in his arms.

"Sleep, little one," he commanded as he removed his thick joint from my ass and rolled over.

I fell right to sleep, dreaming of a dark wizard standing on a high cliff. He kept his wand raised to the stormy sky and repeatedly slashed it through the air, casting spell after spell. White sparks flew from his wand repeatedly, lighting the dark sky and then disappearing.

I woke around five o'clock with Master's giant serpent throbbing away behind me. I realized that in my dream the casting of the spell was probably an undulation of his prick. His soft snoring behind me made me smile as I slowly moved my ass forward and off of his thick shaft.

I loved that I was able to sandwich his cock between my buns as I moved my ass back and forth. The only consolation to not waking up with Master inside me was that I was about to have him down my throat, so I twisted around on the bed and moved under the covers.

It was hot and steamy under the covers. My Master was a big hairy man in his prime and his body was mine for the taking. As usual, his giant phallus was hard as a tree limb and hot to the touch. It was pressed against his hairy stomach, so I pulled it down and guided it into my mouth. My lips closed around his sensitive skin.

"Gage," he said with a deep husky voice.

I took a long drawing pull off of his cock and said, "Master."

"You may continue," he said, like I was doing the most mundane of chores.

"Thank you, Master," I said before impaling myself back onto his fuck stick and starting to blow.

My jaw was sore by the time I finished, but I had a stomach full of Master's seed and I couldn't have been happier.

"Goddamn!" he said as he pulled me up from beneath the covers. "You are fucking spoiling me, little one."

"Just doing my job, Master."

"Well, you are fucking brilliant at your job, Gage. You might be my best worker."

"Might be?" I asked, offended. An image of Vesely sucking on my Master's big cock popped into my head immediately.

We had yet to talk about my punishment, but I was pleased as punch that it had turned out the way it had. Vesely had left with his tail between his legs after not being able to take my Master's cock, while I had been fully impaled on the coven Master's pike. Master seemed to have forgotten the punishment and Vesely already.

"We will see how you perform tonight under the black moon, little one," he said as he popped my bare ass hard making me wince.

I was able to take my Master's giant sword in its entirety, but that didn't mean that I wouldn't pay the price for it for the next twelve hours or so. My asshole felt like I had been fucked with a telephone pole. I scrambled out of bed and waited for my Master.

"You will clean me in the shower and I will do the same for you, Servant," he said as he sat up on the edge of the bed. He looked out the window and said, "It is almost time to gather."

After a shower where I worshipped Master's body one part at a time with a soapy washcloth, we were soon clean and ready to go. He had forbidden me to suck on him or tease his cock while we showered, so I had to just delight in letting my eyes memorize the details of him. He had cleaned me like I was his prized possession, taking time to be gentle but thorough with me. My Master made me feel very safe and special—something that I have not had for the last four years. I wanted to belong to him forever.

I stood naked in the bedroom while Master pulled on a pair of jeans. I figured that I was going to be naked for most of this ceremony anyway, so it didn't bother me to not have clothes on now. Master looked smoking hot with his hairy chest, bare feet, and tatted arms. I loved how expressive his dark brown eyes were when he looked at me.

"What?" he asked finally.

"You are so hot, Master. I catch myself staring at you all the time. I know it must be annoying to you."

"It is flattering, little one. I love that you like me so much. Although changing my appearance constantly is freaking the others out a little bit," he said with a chuckle.

"We will just have to stay together more so that you are consistently smoking hot, Master," I suggested.

He laughed and said, "I am already spending more time

with you than I have with anyone in the last five years combined. It is concerning to the others, although I don't really give a damn what they think."

"I am honored, Master."

"You will be honored tonight, Servant. Let's go," he said as he put an oversized hand around the back of my neck and propelled me forward toward the door. "I'll be lucky to spend the rest of my life honoring you."

The rest of his life . . .

The warlocks and Servants ate quickly and quietly. My Master told me that we had to wait until about eleven thirty to set up because the black moon would be at its height at midnight.

At twenty after eleven, Master stood and announced, "Brothers, tonight we do great work."

The warlocks banged their metal cups on the tops of the tables.

The coven Master continued, "Tonight we try to locate an evil force that has been at play for too long. For years we have been treating the symptoms while the underlying disease has been allowed to fester."

I was very curious about what my Master was referring to. I tried to read between the lines but was still lost.

"Not that we haven't profited from these treatments," Master said with a joking tone. He reached out with his hand in the direction where all the Servants were seated except for me. I ate at the place of honor beside the coven Master and the senior leadership of the gang.

The assembled warlocks laughed.

"But tonight we try to find the ones who have sent our Servants into slavery. Tonight we seek out those that have harmed the marked men that we haven't even rescued yet. Tonight, we help all of the marked men feel safer and shut these scum down forever."

Wow! My Master is going to find the men who had me

kidnapped . . .

Master reached down and grabbed me by the scruff of my neck and pulled me to a standing position beside him. He leaned down and whispered in my ear, "Tonight we are going to find those bastards that took you, Gage." The sharp hairs of his beard tickled the sensitive skin of my ear.

I nodded to him that I understood. My erect dick probably told him even more.

The warlocks clapped and cheered. They slowly started to leave the dining hall and filtered out into the woods. Each warlock was dressed just like Master, naked except jeans. Each Servant was naked except for the red cloaks around their shoulders. I was completely naked.

"You have a question, little one?" Master asked me without even taking his eyes off of the exiting gang members.

"What will we do to them after we find them, Master?"

Master looked down at me and answered, "We will let the authorities know where to find them. Trust me, I would like to do more, but we have a sacred stance toward life. It is not in our nature to do bad things, even to bad people. The energy of all life forces is important to us."

"But you have the power to punish them, don't you, Master?" As soon as I asked this, I wished that I had not.

Master's face looked hurt for a few seconds and then went right back to looking neutral again. "We do," he answered simply.

I did appreciate that about my new Master. I couldn't be entirely bitter toward the men who took me because it had led to me finding my true Master, but I did want them to suffer and pay for what they had done to me. It would be a long time before I felt like I could forgive them. I had spent the last four years remembering every detail and memorizing every face that I could recall. I would not forgive them so soon.

"Let's go make great magic, little one," Master said excitedly as he put his hot hand on the small of my back and nudged me toward the door.

I still wasn't sure what was going to happen or how, but I followed the others out to the compass round. The fire pit was piled high with fresh cut wood and pine boughs. There was what looked like several stacks of twin mattresses off to the side.

"It is your honor to use the besom," Master said to me, loud enough for everyone to hear as he handed me a broom. It was very old and obviously well-taken care of.

A voice called from across the circle. "Master . . ."

I knew it was Stephan without even looking.

I watched my Master as he scanned the other side of the circle. "What is it?" Master asked grumpily.

Stephan spoke loudly and clearly, "It is the head Servant's honor to use the besom, Master."

"Who do you think that is now, Stephan?" Master challenged him.

Stephan looked aghast with disbelief. "There is no thought required, Master. It is me."

"Correction. It *was* you. Now it is Dart."

"But I have been here the longest," Stephan whined. "The head Servant is the one who has the most seniority."

Master looked confident as he said, "The Trad Grimoud clearly says that the head Servant is picked on seniority until such time as the coven Master picks a Servant of his own."

Stephan looked like he had just been punched in the stomach and slapped across the face at the same time. "I am unable to read that book, so I will have to take your word for it, Master."

"Of course you will take my word for it, Servant. I am your Master," the coven leader snapped at Stephan. "Or you could take Dart's word for it, since he is able to read the book."

The warlocks and Servants started to whisper and murmur to each other. Most of them seemed shocked at what the Master was saying.

My Master's voice softened and he said, "Do I speak the truth, Sloven?"

"The Master speaks the truth," Sloven answered immediately. "It is what the book says. I have read it."

"Your honor, Dart," Master said again with pride in his voice. He held out the broom and I reached for it, unsure of what to do next.

"You metaphorically sweep out the bane or bad energy with it," he whispered to me. "Do not actually let it touch the dirt."

I nodded that I understood his instructions and turned to follow them. I was very aware of everyone's eyes on me as I went around the circle sweeping the air. I knew without looking that Stephan was judging me harder than any other.

When I came full circle back to my Master, he took the broom from me and told me that I had done a good job. He signaled to the others who immediately started to move the mattresses into place around the fire pit. The twin mattresses radiated out like the petals of a daisy.

There was no doubt in my mind what was going to happen on those mattresses tonight. I got a special thrill knowing that my Master was going to take me right there in front of everybody. My cock hardened immediately.

Master noticed, of course. He noticed everything. "Excited, little one?" he asked.

"Yes, Master." I couldn't help but smile.

"We locate the men who wronged you tonight. You will get your revenge on them."

I had never thought of it as revenge before. I just did not want them to continue to take boys like me and get away with it. I just wanted to stop them from hurting anyone else.

Or at least, that is what I told myself.

CHAPTER FOURTEEN

A listing of potential targets made by the coven Master and Senior Council of the Warlock Motorcycle Gang on the morning of April eleventh, two thousand and nineteen.

The following groups or individuals have drawn our attention and will be targeted by our spells at upcoming ceremonies in the spring and early summer. The order and spell casting will be left up to the Master.

The men responsible for kidnapping young marked men from the United States and selling them to the highest bidders in Russia.
The Russian military for corruption.
The Bratva or Russian mafia for trafficking in marked men.
The Brigada Oaraza for selling drugs in Northern Italy.
The Gigi Corsicanu clan for being involved in illegal prostitution.
The Feraru clan for robberies in Spain.
The Vasile clan for racketeering operations in Romania and Italy.
The Triads of China for drug trafficking
The Yakuza of Japan for dealing in illegal prostitution.
Kim Jong-un for crimes against humanity
Vladimir Putin for crimes against sexual minorities and for interference in world-wide political elections.

At ten seconds before midnight, my Master ran his hands

through the smoke of the fire. He conjured numbers made from the smoke that hovered and pulsed inside the column rising up from the fire. They counted down from ten to one, along with all the warlocks.

I was naked and on all fours riding a twin mattress. The heat from the large fire was intense and both Master and I were already sweating. He was now naked also, just like everyone else and I was ready to receive him. Master clutched something in each hand, but I was unsure what it was or why he held them. The sides of all of the mattresses contained bowls or jars with various herbs, leaves, or liquids. I had no clue what was going on with these except I knew enough to know that they would be used for magic tonight.

Three. Two. One.

At the end of one, my true Master pushed his giant cockhead into my anal ring. My asshole didn't immediately open for him which caused him to push it into me a good ways before it relented and allowed him access. My anal ring finally flew open and his hot flesh poured inside me like molten steel — painfully hot and burning everything in his path. My ass was made for Master's cock, but that didn't mean that I didn't struggle with his tremendous size and girth each and every time we fucked.

I could hear the moan of satisfaction escape Master's lips as he continued to push his big manhood inside me and I opened for him like a flower receiving a bee's stinger. But my true Master was the biggest, widest bee every seen in nature.

"So tight for me, little one . . ."

My head hung between my shoulders as I dealt with the pain of Master's entry. Every muscle and nerve in my body wanted to tense and freeze in place, but I willed them to stay loose and fluid. The pain was intense and immediate, but I also knew that it wouldn't last long. It would soon turn to exquisite pleasure that rivaled any that I had experienced before. I associated my Master's dick with both pain and pleasure. It was exactly as I would have had it. I wanted nothing more than the sheer fragile balance of both of these feelings.

Master slammed the last of himself into me and the amazing feeling of our coupling overwhelmed me. I felt the blue energy leave us before I saw it. It radiated out from my ass and Master's crotch like a spectacular firework. Usually the blue energy hesitated for a second or two and moved out in a concentric circle from us, but this time it just stayed surrounding the fire pit and all of the men engaged in sex within.

I studied the blue energy since it held steady in the air around us. It was anything but motionless, its parts seemed to constantly move around inside itself. There was also another light coming from behind me — one that was golden in color.

When I twisted my neck to try to see where the golden light was coming from, Master stroked his palm down the middle of my back and said, "It is my mark, little one."

"Your mark, Master?"

"It is glowing."

I didn't have a lot of time to think about why the claiming mark was glowing or why the blue energy ring was acting abnormally because my Master's cock was very insistently demanding my attention. It was throbbing inside me like a snake trapped in a pipe. His big cock felt like it was made to be inside my ass, but there was always a question about whether it would fit at any given time.

I turned to look at my Master, but his eyes were closed. He looked like he might have been in a trance, but within a few seconds, his hips and lips started to move. He kept his eyes closed, but his cock knew the way to tear up my ass anyway. He slammed into me until his short pubic hairs tickled my ass cheeks with each thrust.

Master fucked me hard, harder than he ever had before, and I hadn't thought that was possible. When I was able to lift my head, I could see the other warlocks doing the same thing around the circle, even though it was hard to focus on anything while Master worked my ass over. The other marked men in the circle were being tore up just like me.

A noise brought my attention to something next to one of the trees. I watched in fascination as several buckets began to vibrate where they sat on the ground. Magically, the buckets lifted off of the ground and moved toward the men on the mattresses. I quickly looked to my side to see a bucket coming right for me and Master.

Ducking, I saw that the bucket moved above me where I couldn't see it anymore, so I watched what was happening to the others. The buckets stopped above the men and then tilted. I felt the cold water at the same time that I saw it happen to the others. I was so hot that the water was an instant relief for me. I was sure that Master felt the same way, although he didn't even twitch or open his eyes. The water poured off of me taking my sweat with it. My hair was soaked.

Suddenly an image appeared, hovering above the fire pit. I watched in fascination as the image got more and more defined. The image coalesced into the shape of a globe which began to spin. I could make out the countries and the oceans in the image.

Master increased the pace of his rhythm and red dots appeared on the globe. We were both sweating profusely — some from the heat of the fire and mostly from the heat of the sex. I loved the feel of Master's sweaty palms on my hips.

"It's working," Master called out loudly. His voice startled me in the silence of the woods. His eyes were open now, but his gaze was distant. "Drive deep, brothers," he urged.

A series of grunts and moans rose up from the mattresses as the warlocks increased their efforts. My ass felt like it was on fire from the friction. Master was punching into me in places that he had never reached before and I was practically delirious with the combination of pleasure and pain. My dick was so hard that it was painful, but when I realized that Master had gone to his feet on either side of my hips and was now crouched over my ass, my cock went to a whole new level of hardness.

Thankfully, another set of buckets came flying over us and drenched me with their cold contents. We were so hot that I was pretty sure that some of it turned to steam as it hit our bodies. This time I held my head back and my mouth open to get some of the water into my dry mouth.

The globe stopped spinning and became a flat map. I recognized it as the United States and another country that looked like it was somewhere in Europe. The map began to zoom in over and over again and it didn't take me long to realize that each of Master's thrusts into me was causing the change. It made me feel like I was causing the zoom to happen which gave me a wonderful feeling of being part of the magic that was taking place.

I couldn't take the pressure anymore. My cock was so hard and I needed release so badly. I could feel my climax building in my nuts and working out and up my shaft. It felt like my prick was a giant thermometer from a cartoon with the top bulging red. I was going to blow all over this mattress while my Master happily banged away deep inside my ass like a miner looking for the mother lode.

"Not yet, little one," he said behind me firmly. His voice was husky and otherworldly. "Wait for me."

How does he know? Are our bodies so synced with each other's that now we can feel what is happening inside the other's body? I didn't think it was possible to stop the tidal wave that was threatening to overwhelm me, but I willed it to.

Each red dot shimmering on the map got larger and more defined as we zoomed in. I could see now that there were six red dots in the smoke. Three of them were in the United States—it looked like one was in Ohio and two were in New York City. The other three were in the other country which now looked to me like Bulgaria.

A red-hot streak ran through my balls and up my spine. Master was close to his release. I could feel it suddenly just like he must have been able to feel mine. He was ready to fall over the cliff and I was already standing on the ledge.

The map zoomed in again as Master thrust into me and then again. We were now past the state maps and the smoke was forming into a city. Master was trying to identify where the men that took me were located so that he could report them to the police. In order for the police to find them, he had to know where to say to search.

Two more thrusts and the shimmering red dots suddenly formed into shapes of men. Two more quick thrusts gave the dots faces and suddenly I saw the men who had kidnapped me four years ago. The faces from my nightmares were there in glaring red smoke.

It was shocking to see the faces of the men whom I had spent four years hating. Faces I had forced myself to remember every single detail of were now emblazoned in front of me. A bitter hatred rose up from me at the sight of those faces. I could taste it in my mouth. Suddenly I was the one thrusting back onto my Master's long prong.

"Fuuuuccccckkkkk," Master hissed between clenched teeth.

I wanted to see the images of the men. I wanted to be the one to get my revenge. My hips and legs were burning from the night's efforts, but I found a reserve of adrenaline that caused me to hum back and forth on Master like a piston in a souped-up race car. I was surprised by how quickly and strongly the hatred had risen out of me.

"Gage," Master said in a whisper.

"Master," I said as I hit my release. I couldn't hold it anymore and neither could he.

Master and I both lost our shit as my arms collapsed and my head hit the mattress. My cum vent opened and I pumped a huge load of strong-smelling spunk onto the mattress while my cheek was pressed onto it. I moaned shamelessly as I surrendered to it. There were just two things in the world — my cock and the one buried deep inside me, both of them pumping strand after strand of hot cum out of them.

The fire burning in my ass was soon squelched by Master's big load as he continued to pump it inside me. He shook and jerked with his release, holding onto my hips to keep from falling on top of me. In this moment, he was totally one with me.

After a minute, I had never felt such a flood of relief before in my whole life. I lay silent except for my heavy breathing. My cock stilled and so did the one inside of me.

Someone asked loudly, "What the fuck just happened?"

I recognized it as Sloven's voice. He was on the mattress located beside Master and me.

My Master's deep voice answered, "I don't know. That was not in the plan."

Now I was curious about what they were talking, but not so curious that I had to move. I was absolutely exhausted from the fuck that Master had just given me. I could tell there was confusion amongst the warlocks, because I could hear muffled talk above the crackling of the fire.

"Let's reset and try again," Master said firmly. "I'm not sure what happened, but we might be able to tell if we start again."

Start again? He is going to fuck me again just like he had? I didn't know whether that news brought me sheer delight or unbelievable disbelief, but I was more than willing to find out. It felt like my ass had been destroyed, but there was no way that I wasn't going to do it all over again.

"You are exhausted, Dart?" Master asked me as he leaned over and looked down at me.

"I am always here for you, Master."

"Yes, you are, but you are tired."

"Yes, Master."

"Your Master will take it easy on you this time."

"Please don't, Master," I said softly.

The big coven Master chuckled and asked, "So hungry for me, aren't you, little one?"

"Always, my Master."

"I just meant that I'm going to allow you to sit on my big pole this time and that I would do all the work, little one."

"Thank you, Master. You always know what is best for me."

"That I do," he told me as he slowly pulled his still-hard dick out of my sore ass.

He knelt down, picked me up, and flipped me over onto my back. Master sat down on the mattress and spread his legs. He leaned forward and easily lifted me into his strong arms.

"Something amazing just happened, Gage," he whispered to me as he pressed me to his chest.

"What was it, Master?"

Master began to tell me as if I had not witnessed any of it, "We were able to locate the men who kidnapped you four years ago. We had located their positions and started to see their faces. Then, something happened. Something I had not planned for and had not seen coming."

"What happened, Master?"

He smiled down at me and asked, "You know that blue energy ring that comes out of us when I push my prick all the way inside you?"

I nodded that I did.

"It was hovering around the scene the whole time we were conjuring and then the blue ring suddenly developed into six blue spikes."

I was not shocked to hear this. I had seen the ring become my father the first time that my Master had nailed me. That blue image of my Dad even walked and talked.

"The six blue spikes shot like rockets into the hearts of the images of the six red men that we had conjured."

I had not expected that. "And what happened, Master?"

"I don't know," he answered distantly. "The whole scene just disappeared right in front of us."

"And that is why we need to reset the scene, Master?"

"When I am inside you, anything is possible, little one."

"I want you inside me all the time, Master," I told him as I lay my head on his shoulder.

"Lucky me," he said before pushing his mighty staff back inside me again. He held me with one hand in the small of my back while he lowered my ass down onto his ever-hard prong with the other.

Even though my asshole was sore, it opened to him like a flower on a bright sunny day. His hot flesh inside me felt like it belonged there. As if it had always been meant to be there, but was temporarily missing. He plowed through my cum-drenched chamber until he was fully inserted inside me again.

"That's where I like to be," he groaned into the side of my face as he settled me down onto his lap. I was facing him and the heat from his hairy chest had instantly heated my smooth one.

I opened my eyes to see the familiar blue ring of energy emanate out from Master and me. This time it did not stay around but quickly spread out from us in a larger and larger circle until it was lost in the deep black of the forest.

Master reached down and grabbed some things out of the containers on the sides of the mattress. "Hush now, little one. We have great work to do."

I closed my eyes again as Master started to slowly clench and unclench his ass muscles—driving his fat cock further up into me and then pulling it slowly back out of me. I'm not sure if I fell asleep from exhaustion or was lulled into some kind of trance, but I lost all sense of time.

The next thing that I became aware of was my Master talking.

"That can't be right." His deep voiced boomed across the compass round.

One of the warlock's voices called, "How can they be here?"

"What is it, Master?" I asked, suddenly afraid.

"The spell is saying that the men that we are trying to locate are here in Romania now, Dart."

Fuck! Were they after me again?

Chapter Fifteen

Part of an official FBI report filed at their headquarters in Quantico, Virginia on the morning of April eleventh, 2019.

Our Midwest field team reports a strange occurrence in a case which they have been involved. Normally, it would not be reportable to the headquarters, but the New York City office has reported the same strange occurrence in their branch of the same investigation.

The Midwest team was tracking a series of missing marked men in Ohio. The string of men missing could be traced to Kentucky, Tennessee, North Carolina, South Carolina, and Georgia dating from at least the last five years. Rumors persist on the street that the men responsible are connected to various mafia organizations in Western Europe.

The perp in Ohio, a Bulgarian national by the name of Igor Stravkosky, was working out of an abandoned warehouse in the garment district in downtown Cleveland. The field operatives were able to videotape him from across the street and recorded multiple phone conversations from the building.

In the middle of a call to his contacts in New York City, he simply vanished. The phone was found on the floor of the building when the operatives raided it, the line still connected. The Midwest operatives had the New York agents raid the known offices of his contacts and they also were missing.

The offices of the New York perps were left just like they were there and left in a hurry — water on to boil, a frozen pizza in the oven, the TV on in the middle of a movie, and a cell phone in the middle of the floor. The phone was still connected to the call placed from the Ohio perp's cellphone.

No camera footage caught the perps leaving the buildings and no field agents saw them either. There has been no flash traffic to the numbers in Bulgaria that they have called in the past.

Whereabouts still unknown.

A breaking voice called from behind me, "Master!"

I opened my eyes from where my head was lying on the Master's shoulder. I was sitting on his lap and facing toward the forest while he was facing the compass round, so I was in the best position to see what was happening behind him. His fat cock kept me grounded to his lap like a plastic figure on top of a birthday cake. I lifted my head to be able to see more easily.

The coven Master made a grumbling sound as he continuously thrust his fat cock inside me. It was not a happy sound, even though I was pretty sure that he was doing his favorite activity. He was in the middle of casting a spell and he was being interrupted again.

The voice called again. "Master!"

I wasn't able to see the owner of the voice, but I could hear him coming closer through the underbrush. I saw the light bouncing through the trees first. When the man finally stepped out, I recognized him as one of the seekers from camp—a warlock in training. He was holding a torch, making him resemble a medieval squire.

"What is it?" Master snapped. "You know we are not supposed to be disturbed at the black moon!"

"I-I know, Master. Sorry, Master, but . . ."

"Spit it out, Henrik," he ordered firmly. "Dart's sweet ass will not wait while you ramble on."

I didn't know how my Master knew which seeker this was without looking at him, but he did. And I wasn't sure that he was correct about my ass, because I believed that his cock, which was throbbing away inside me, was the impatient one. I had seen Henrik around the camp but had never spoken to him. There were three or four seekers in the Warlock camp.

"We have company, Master," Henrik finally said. "The other seekers and I heard something. We were in the meeting room when we heard a loud sound outside."

"What type of sound?"

"It was like a very loud popping sound, Master."

"You are holding something back, Henrik. Out with it."

I was constantly amazed by how my Master could know the things that he did. He seemed to always be right when he said things like this.

Henrik stumbled with his words before they came flowing out. "Some of the others said that it was the same sound that came when your hot tub arrived in camp, Master."

I felt the big man's body tense, but his cock relentlessly pounded away deep inside me. I wished that I knew what he was thinking. "Who is it that comes in the middle of the night, Henrik?"

"I-I-I don't know them, Master," Henrik finally said after stuttering over his answer. I wondered if he was afraid of disappointing the Master with his answer or just plain scared of him. My new Master did not have the friendliest of relationships with many of his men like he had with me.

The whole compass round was completely quiet as they listened to the conversation happening near me. I looked over my shoulder and saw, unlike Master and I, that the others had stopped fucking. Their naked sweaty bodies were frozen in mid-fuck like they had been turned to stone.

"Are we in danger, Henrik?" Master asked evenly.

Henrik actually snorted before answering, "No, Master. I'm pretty sure that they are not harmful to us."

"Then attend to the guests and we will be there shortly," Master commanded. "Dart here needs my cock's full attention some more before I am done. And we only have another hour or so of magical time during the black moon."

Henrik hesitated.

Sloven seized on the seeker's hesitation, saying, "I can go see who it is, Master."

"Thank you, Sloven, but I have a pretty good idea who our visitors are and if they are contained, then they can definitely wait until after we finish here."

Sloven asked the same question aloud that I was thinking to myself. "What if Henrik is wrong about whether they are a threat to us or not, Master? I mean, no offense, but he is in training."

"I will consider your concerns, Slo. Leave us, Henrik. Make sure that the visitors are watched but not spoken to."

Henrik's dark eyes flicked to my face before settling again on the back of my Master's head. "Yes, Master." I watched Henrik turn and disappear into the woods. He seemed to be in a hurry.

The coven Master thrust into me five or six more times. I wouldn't call them angry thrusts, but he was definitely more aggressive in his fucking style than before. Finally, he held me still before whispering into my ear, "What would you do, little one."

"I will bend to your wishes, Master."

"You will always bend to my wishes, Gage. But if I insisted that you answer?"

"I want to see them, Master."

"You have the same idea of who they are that I do, Gage?" Master asked sounding impressed.

"It would make sense, Master," I answered him.

"You constantly surprise me, little one."

"I hope that I will always continue to, Master."

Master's deep voice rang out in the small clearing, "Boys, our spell has been disrupted by multiple forces tonight. We will try again tomorrow night. Enjoy your marked men, and I will see you in the morning. Dart, by the very fact that he is mounted on my dick, will of course be going with me."

"Would you like me to come with you, Master?" Sloven asked from the mattress beside ours.

"No, Slo. You finish long-dicking Teo there, and I will call for you if I need you. We will probably have to have a leadership meeting concerning this as soon as you guys return to camp."

"Are you sure, Master?" Sloven asked with concern in his voice.

"Don't question me, Sloven," Master said in a tone which told everyone to keep their mouths closed from then on.

My true Master leaned forward, making sure to hold me clasped to his chest with one arm before standing up. I had never seen a man who could so easily control his body and mine while we were fucking, like this one could. Master stood up and turned to walk back to the camp. His thick cock was still spreading me open.

He growled into my ear, "I am not finished with you yet, little one."

"Nor I, you, Master," I said back.

"I want you swimming in my cum tonight."

I felt like I already was from the one huge load he had deposited inside me. "I am yours to do with what you want, Master."

"Of course, you are." Master stepped into the woods away from the compass round. He easily took a few more steps until we were completely alone. "And I want to finish fucking you right now," he said as he planted my back against the wide trunk of a pine tree near the path.

The sharp bark cut into my back as Master positioned me

onto the wide trunk of the tree and began to hunch up inside of me. I wrapped my arms around his thick neck and rode each one of his thrusts up and down the front of him. He was aggressive like a bull in his prime, and my cock hardened in response to him. He was everything that I had wanted in a man and didn't even realize it.

"You ... do ... something ... to ... me, Gage," Master grunted between each hard thrust inside me.

"And you're doing just what I want you to do to me, Master," I said between each forward movement of his big hairy chest. "It's what I need you to do." I held onto his sweaty biceps as he finished us off. My Master collapsed onto me, pinning me to the tree. I moved my hands around his thick neck and clung to him.

I came with another monumental climax that left me feeling more drained than I thought possible. My cum shot onto Master's hairy chest and matted it like a plaster cast. I was spent.

Master's release truly had me swimming in his cum. When he regained his breath, he gently leaned back from the tree which lifted me off of it. He looked at me with amazement in his eyes.

I wanted to ask him why he looked so surprised, but I just did not have the energy left to do so. He turned us around so that I was able to see the pine tree where he had just mounted me.

It was metal. The tree was fucking metal. I could tell from the occasional glint of moonlight off of the trunk that it was silver and shiny. Master moved us closer and I felt it. It was definitely metal.

"I think its pewter," Master said with awe.

"The whole tree, Master?"

"I thought it was just a covering at first, but it seems solid. That fuck was amazing enough to turn a whole tree," he said, staring down at me. He lowered me to the forest floor and I caught myself on shaky legs. It was the first time in a while that his big cock had not been stretching my anal ring wide open, so it felt really weird.

"It was," I agreed, trying not to wince from the pain of standing. My ass felt like it was on fire. "Master, I don't think I can walk right now," I admitted to the big man. My ass was not only burning but there was a sharp pain deep inside me that I did not want to experience if I didn't have to.

"My bad," he said as he reached down and lifted me easily into his arms. "I shouldn't have been so rough."

"Bullshit! I wanted you to be rough. Don't ever back off, Master."

"You telling me what to do, little one?" he asked as he started to walk through the woods carrying me.

"I am yours to do with what you want, Master."

"You bet your ass you are." He took a few steps and then added, "You and I are going to do amazing things, Gage."

"I will do whatever you want, Master."

"You like me that much, little one?"

"You are my true Master. I have one job and that is to bring you pleasure and that is what I will do until you won't have me anymore."

He chuckled and said, "That may not be for a very long time."

"Let's hope, Master."

The coven Master stepped out of the woods and into the campsite still cradling me in his arms. Henrik was waiting for him with a lit torch.

"Master!" he said, rushing up to us. He immediately lowered his head and said, "Dart, I am sorry that I interrupted your time with the Master."

"It's all right, Henrik," I told him. "The Master and I will make up for lost time later." Henrik's expressions were exaggerated by the light from the torch he was holding.

"You can count on that," Master said gruffly. "Where are the visitors, Henrik? Why aren't you watching them?"

"They are right over here near your new hot tub, Master. I don't think they need watching."

"I don't have you in training to think for yourself, Henrik. You should be more cautious."

"Yes, Master," Henrik said flatly.

Master looked down at me with another curious look on his face and then started to walk toward our cabin. How he could see in the complete darkness of the night was still a mystery to me.

He confidently strode up to our cabin and then walked to the left side of the clearing. I could see that something was illuminated there. My eyes adjusted to the brighter lights, making out the shape of the new hot tub. Master lowered me down to the ground but held me to his side. I was grateful that we remained in physical contact with each other.

Suddenly, I saw a row of cages and then movement inside. My eyes adjusted to the light and my shock subsided so that I could count six cages, each with a man inside.

"Get us the fuck out of here!" one of the men yelled.

"What did you bastards do to us?"

"Help us!"

Their accents were heavy with what I thought might be some type of Eastern European accents. They were aggressive and started to rush the front bars of the cages.

"Silence!" Master said firmly as he raised his hand to them.

All sound ceased immediately. I recognized the men a second later.

"These are the men that took you four years ago, Dart?" Master asked me solemnly.

How the fuck?

"Yes, Master."

CHAPTER SIXTEEN

Part of a journal entry made by Gage, the coven Master's Servant on the morning of the twelfth of April, 2019.

I don't know what forces were at work to have led me to this point in my life, but I will be forever grateful to them. I have found the man of my dreams. And not only have I found him, but he seems to be as interested in me as I am in him.

The man has turned out to be a very powerful man—a man of magic, a leader of his people, someone who others look up to, someone who others envy, a man of many secrets. He is everything that I wanted in a man and so much more that I didn't even know could exist in a man.

Not only do I click with this man, but he is my true Master. I knew it from the very moment I saw him and it was confirmed for me the second he pushed that big cock of his inside me. Not only did he make me his Servant, but he admits that he is my true Master. He feels the same pull and draw to me that I feel toward him.

Never have I met a man like him before. He is my whole world-absolute and without thought. I will do anything that he asks of me and I will enjoy bringing him pleasure in any form that he desires. He is not a man who would abuse that power, but rather the rare one who would share that power with me. We are equals, yet he is my Master. We both have power, yet he has complete command of me.

He has rescued me from my prison, he has found the men that have wronged me, and now he is punishing them. I haven't asked him to do this nor dropped any hints that this is something that I wanted him to do. He is just in-tune with me.

I think I am falling in love with him, and I still don't know his name.

"What the fuck?" I asked aloud as I looked at my former captors, now captive themselves.

My Master growled at me.

"Sorry, Master. What the fuck, Master?" I asked, correcting myself.

"Do you recognize them, little one?"

"Some of them, Master."

"You expected it to be them?" he asked, looking down at me.

"I thought it made logical sense that it was them when you described to me what had happened with the blue energy ring and the spell, Master."

"Me too. Your desire must have been to see them again?"

"Yes, sir."

"And mine was to have them be punished — to cage them like they did you and to treat them like nothing more than the animals they are."

I chuckled and said, "Well, we both got our desires fulfilled, Master. Thanks, blue energy ring."

"I guess we should coordinate our desires before fucking in the future," he said with a smirk on his face.

"Usually my desire is to just be fucked by you, Master."

"Thank the spirit world for that!" he said with a smile.

"Now, what do we do with them, Master?"

"I'm not sure," he said before turning to Henrik. "What did they say to you before we got here, Henrik?"

"They said that they couldn't move off of all-fours, Master and that they want to be released, of course. They say that they have done nothing wrong, but we all know how that goes. Are these the men that took you, Dart?"

I nodded to answer the young seeker.

"They are compelled to be in an animal position," Master thought aloud. "It's very interesting magic."

"Will you let them speak, Master?" I asked.

He looked down at me and asked, "Do you have things to say to them, little one?"

"Yes, sir."

"Very well. Henrik, you may leave us now," he commanded.

Henrik promptly left after acknowledging his Master's orders.

The coven Master raised his hand and all of the men in the cages choked or coughed. "You will be respectful," he warned in a menacing tone. "My Servant would like to speak with you. If you are not respectful to him, I will make sure that you regret it."

One of them who looked dark and surly rubbed his throat and asked, "What the fuck are you guys?"

"We are your Masters from now on," my Master answered.

"The marked one we know," one of the others said.

I recognized the speaker immediately as the man that I was attracted to four years ago when I followed him into a dark alley. His gaze never left mine as he talked, giving me a cold chill.

"No shit," I shot back in reply. "The six of you put me through hell, and now I'm turning the tables on you."

"It was just business," the surly one said.

Another one with a heavy accent added, "You're a cock-sucker. It's what you do. We just made sure that you had a lot of cocks to suck."

"Fuck you!" Master spit. He reached down and grabbed a stick off of the ground and bowed his head over it.

The one who had called me the name screamed and lurched forward in the cage, smashing his face against the bars.

"I warned you to be respectful," Master growled, now looking up. "Are you going to play nice now?"

"Yes," the man said in anguish, while trying to nod his head against the bars.

"Did you ram that stick up his butt, Master?" I whispered.

"I sure did and I will do it to the next one who offends you, Dart." He said this more to the men in the cages than to me.

"That is not the name we knew him by," the handsome one said, still staring at me.

"It is the name given to me by the men to whom you sold me," I said, feeling no need to really explain it to them.

"It was just business," the surly man repeated.

"Illegal business," Master corrected him. "You are a sex slave trafficker and by the end of your time here with us you will wish that the cops had found you instead of us."

"What are you going to do to us?" one of the others asked.

"Anything I want," Master snapped. "Which ones of you violated my Servant here four years ago before you sold him into slavery?"

I immediately knew the answer to his question. Both men attempted to raise their hands but were unable. They admitted it verbally instead. Master checked with me and I nodded to him. They both cringed as if they were waiting for the terrible pain to arrive that had visited their colleague.

Master stepped toward the cages and announced, "Tomorrow, you two will be forced to suck Dart's cock and then will have the pleasure of being fucked by him."

"And the rest of us?"

"You will find out shortly."

The surly one, who seemed to be the leader said, "I understand the revenge that you want to have on us. We have done terrible things for money, but I do not understand what you have done to us so that we cannot move. And how did we get here?"

"We are warlocks," the coven Master explained.

"Like you can do magic?"

"Can you move out of that position?" Master asked, challenging him.

"No," the leader answered grumpily.

"Even the sperm burper?" the man pressed against the bars spat out at Master while he stared at me.

My Master bowed his head and shoved the stick further up the man's ass as he screamed bloody murder. When he stopped, the man in the cage slumped onto the floor against the bars breathing hard.

"I guess some of you are unable to learn how to be civil. Your path is going to be extremely painful," Master promised the man.

"I would like him to try to take your big cock, Master," I said suddenly.

"Don't worry, little one. That man is going to be ripped wide open by me very shortly."

"You made a very big mistake in selling Dart. You didn't know what you had, of course. He has the most magic of all of us," Master told the men held captive in the cages. "And you will never disrespect him again," he said with a wave of his hand.

The hateful kidnapper's body lurched forward as he rammed his face into the bars of his cage. His nose broke and blood started to pour down his face. Master waved again and the man rammed his face into the bars again.

"Okay, okay!" the man howled through his pain.

"Apologize to him," Master said after another wave that produced more blood.

"I'm sorry, I'm sorry!" the man yelled.

"We'll see who the cocksucker is tonight," Master promised as he waved his hand and immediately silenced them. "Henrik!" he yelled.

"Yes, Master," the seeker said before stepping out from the front of the house.

"Bring these men water in dog bowls and place it under their heads. They want to act like dogs, then we will treat them like dogs."

"Yes, Master."

Master looked down at me and said, "Sloven and the leadership team are on their way. We will explain what happened and hear their comments. And then I will put you to bed."

"Yes, Master."

Sloven and the leaders of the gang soon joined us. As soon as they came to a stop, they produced more light from their hands.

"Who are these men, Master?" the second in command asked. His face was all curiosity as his eyes took in the whole scene.

"These are the men that we were hunting tonight, Sloven."

"The ones that took Dart and the others?"

"Yes."

One of the other leaders asked, "But how?"

Master turned around and explained our theory to the other warlocks. After all that they had seen over the past few days, it was not such a stretch for them to believe.

"What do we do with them now?" Sloven asked once Master had answered all of the questions the men asked. "I mean, this is not what we do, Master. We have never had captives before."

"We will turn them over to the police after they have been punished," the Master answered.

"How are we to punish them?" Sloven asked.

"We are going to fuck the shit out of them, just like they did to all of those boys they took."

"Can't we just hand them over to the police, Master? I mean, I would love to fuck some tight holed NOMAR, but we don't want to draw attention to ourselves, do we?" Marco asked.

"I don't think we can break the spell until we punish them," Master explained.

They all turned to look at the men in the cages. Jaxon asked, "What's the spell?"

"They seem to be permanently on all fours," I added. When I saw Master's glare, I quickly bowed my head.

"That should make the fucking that much easier," Marco commented with a chuckle.

"Yes, it should," my Master confirmed. "These two are for Dart's use first and then you may have them," Master told the men while pointing out the two captives whom had fucked me so long ago. He walked over to the cage with the bleeding man in it, put his arm across the bars and said, "This one is mine. He is going to feel the full brunt of my sword tomorrow."

"Dart is going to get to fuck them?" Sloven asked with a raised eyebrow and a look of surprise.

"Marked men can fuck just as well as NOMARs, Sloven," I said with attitude.

"Just as well?" Master asked me.

I blushed furiously and admitted, "Well, no one fucks as good as you do, Master."

He chuckled and said, "I didn't think so." He turned back to the leadership of his gang and said, "Sloven, make a chart for feeding, cleaning, and guarding them. I will announce what has happened to the gang."

"Yes, Master."

"Dart and I are going to go rest. We will be in our cabin if you need me."

"Yes, Master."

"Master, can I ask a favor of you?" I asked carefully.

The big man looked down at me, his face a mask of curiosity. "You may, little one."

"Could it be arranged for the other Servants to also have their revenge on these men, Master? I think that would be closure for them as much as it will be for me."

He smiled and said, "Make it happen, Sloven. Any other demands, little one?"

I smiled and answered, "No, Master."

The coven Master reached down and picked me up like I was a feather. He easily held me in his arms as he turned around and walked to the front of our cottage. I saw that the entire camp had gathered there. I was starting to get used to being completely naked in front of them now.

Master easily held me in his arms as he addressed the crowd. "Vrajitors, we performed exceptional magic tonight. We were able to locate the six men who have been kidnapping marked men for years now."

He let that sink in before he took a deep breath and went for it. "The special magic that Dart and I have together allowed us to not only identify the kidnappers but also bring them here to our camp."

There was sudden chatter and sounds of surprise.

Master continued, "They are in cages on the side of my cabin. They are currently under the effects of a very complex spell that causes them to kneel on all fours."

Chuckles rang out through the crowd.

"We will take our revenge on them by fucking their asses until they bleed!" the coven Master yelled out.

A roar went up from the crowd.

"Our marked men will have the day off while we punish

the kidnappers. And then we will turn them over to the authorities."

Another roar went up from the crowd before they began to chant his title over and over.

The coven Master turned around, walked onto the porch, and opened the door without touching it. He carried me straight to the bed.

He whispered to me, "You have done fine work tonight, Gage." After a short pause, he added, "I have never met anyone like you I'm not sure there *is* another like you. You are my equal even though you are my Servant."

"I am yours, Master."

"You are mine," he agreed. "You want to belong to me, don't you, little one?"

"I need it, Master."

"You need me to dominate you . . ."

"Yes, Master."

"You need me to control you . . ."

"I have to bend to your will, Master."

"My will is your desire?"

"Always, my Master."

He lay me down in the bed and said, "Tomorrow night we leave for the United States, little one. Rest up."

"Yes, Master," I said with a yawn. Opening my eyes wider, I said, "Thank you for keeping your promise to me, Master."

"I will always take care of your needs, Gage."

"Of that, I am certain, Master."

"Sleep," he commanded.

He crawled into the bed behind me and pulled my back until I was spooned against his hairy chest. "You will shower and clean yourself first thing tomorrow morning. We have a lot to do before we can leave."

"I will be ready, my Master."

"Yes, you will," he whispered before starting to snore softly into the back of my head.

CHAPTER SEVENTEEN

Part of a letter written by Gage, the coven Master's Servant, to his father in the United States on the morning of the thirteenth of April, 2019.

Dad,

My Master said that we are going to leave tonight to come see you. I'm not sure how long the flight will be, but we should be there by the end of tomorrow I would think.

I'm so excited to see you again and to hear what I have missed for the last four years. I'm also very excited for you to meet my Master. He is truly an amazing man unlike any I have met before. I hope that you will try to get along with him especially since he is such a big part of my life now.

I know that when I was taken, we had never really discussed sex or my marked nature. I want to get that awkwardness out of the way as soon as possible. I am a very sexual being and this man knows exactly what I need when I need it. He is my true Master and I will stay with him for as long as he will have me. As hard as it will be to leave you again after our visit, it pales in comparison to how it would affect me to leave my Master.

You may be disappointed in me for this attitude and stance, but I have wasted too many years already and I will not miss another day. I will not let the most amazing man that I have ever met slip away from me. I would like your blessing in this, even though I know it is hard for you to give. It is what is best for me and what I need.

I hope this letter finds you well and I am overjoyed to finally be able to come home to see you, even if it is only for a visit. Please don't go to any fuss for my homecoming. I wouldn't mind if it was just you and I getting caught up. My Master does not want to draw any attention to either one of us, and I do not want to have to spend my time with reporters or police officers.

Immediately after breakfast, Master asked me which one of the kidnappers I wanted to fuck. I told him that the pretty boy was the one who had seduced me into the alley that had forever changed my life, so I would start with him.

Master ordered me to his cabin and told me to wait on the bed.

I was naked on my back on the bed when I heard the front door open. I had almost forgotten why I was there because I was busy breathing in deeply of my Master's smell. The whole bed smelled like him and it gave me a raging hard-on to be wallowing in it. My nostrils were filled with the smell of honeysuckle and cum when he walked in.

My Master carried the criminal with one big muscled arm around his waist. The man was still on all fours, even though he was in the air looking like a giant stuffed dog. Master sat him down on the floor at the end of the bed and handed me a leash. My gaze followed the strap of leather to the criminal's neck where it was attached to a collar.

"My present to you, little one. Would you mind if I stayed to watch?" he asked.

"I'm afraid my fucking ability doesn't even come close to yours, my Master," I said, feeling my face start to heat.

The big warlock looked down at me fondly. "It doesn't have to, Dart. This is for your closure, not to impress me, or him for that matter."

"You are right, Master."

"Aren't I always?" he asked with a smirk.

"You are always right for me, my Master."

"Yes, I am. So, do you mind if I stay to watch? I see you

are already very excited for it," he said as he reached out and tweaked my hard cock. His smile told me that he was extremely happy for me.

"That is from smelling you in the bed, Master," I quickly corrected him. "I am always in awe of your ability to excite me even when you are not in the room."

He reached up and cupped my face in his oversized hand. His thumb ran back and forth across my cheek. "Do you know how hard it was not to fuck the shit out of you this morning?"

"I wanted you to, Master," I admitted shamefully.

He smiled and said, "I have big plans for us for later. Now, get to work, little one."

"Yes, Master."

I put on a show for my Master, but my heart wasn't into the punishment of these men. I would have much rather been alone in the bed with my Master than getting any revenge.

Master complimented me on my fucking style and my stamina before carrying each man out of my bed. He gave them to the other warlocks to pleasure themselves with. By the end of the day, most of the kidnappers were able to stand for the first time, but were unable to walk due to the fact that they had been stuck in the same position for so long. The coven Master ordered them cuffed, chained to their cages, and guarded at all times.

As soon as the sun set, the seekers arranged torches around the area on the side of our cottage. It was weird to have one side of the house oddly illuminated while the others were in darkness. I assumed the purpose of the torches was to be able to see the captives at night so that they could keep guard duty, but I was wrong.

My Master came to me right after dinner and said, "Gage, I would like to show our captives what they have missed out on by selling you like a piece of cattle."

This statement required no response from me, so I gave him none. I just looked into his face to show him that I was listening.

When he saw that I had digested this much information, he added, "You are the most powerful wizard we have in camp. I would like you and me to show them your power. Would you mind doing that?"

"If you desire it, Master, then I will do it," I answered. I was thrilled to be with him at any time and I knew that our power came from fucking, so I couldn't have been happier to oblige.

"Yes, I know that you will please me, but what I want to know is if you mind getting fucked in front of them." He said it bluntly and waited for my response. When he saw that I wasn't going to respond yet, he added, "I never want to force you to do something that you do not feel comfortable doing and never want you to feel obligated to do it because I want you to do it. Do you understand what I'm trying to say?"

"I would never mind getting fucked by you, Master, no matter who was watching," I answered honestly.

"Excellent!" He smiled and gripped me around the back of my neck with his hot palm. "Now for the better news that I have to tell you, I would like us to teleport to see your father tonight, little one. Can you have that desire in your mind when I enter you?"

I returned his grin. "Yes, sir!"

"Travel to Atlanta, Gage. That is what I want you to be saying to yourself over and over as I fuck you. Can you do that?"

Atlanta? Does my Master not realize that my father lives outside of Charleston? "Yes, Master." I was unable to correct him since he had not given me permission to talk freely. I guessed if we teleported to the wrong location, we could just fuck again and teleport to somewhere else, so I didn't consider the location a big deal.

"I am going to be a little more specific in the location that I desire, Gage, but I want you to focus on Atlanta for me. Can you do that for me? Can you do that for *us*?"

"Yes, sir." I was overjoyed that he had just asked me to do something for *us*. His use of that word was everything to me.

He smiled at my compliance and said, "You are the man. Now, let's go put on a show." He led the way out of the cabin and then put his arm around my waist. We walked side-by-side into the campsite where I saw that everyone from the gang had gathered.

It was going to be a show for everyone, I assumed. I saw that many of the kidnappers were standing outside their cages now, still chained to them by the neck. Many of them looked defeated, but not all. Most of them looked interested to see what was going to happen next.

Master led me into the clearing made by the assembled men where an old mattress had been placed onto the ground. He stopped us right in front of it and held up his arms for silence, which he immediately received. I loved how his men respected him and I vowed to obey him the same way.

"Brothers, last night we worked spectacular magic and we were rewarded for it today." The assembled men laughed out loud while the captives just glared. Master continued, "Tonight, Dart and I are going to show these criminals what awesome power they had in their hands and gave away." He addressed the captives, saying, "You're going to see what tremendous magic this one has when he is properly fucked."

Master turned to me, indicated the mattress with his hand, and said, "My Servant."

"My Master," I said before lying down on the mattress

and waiting for his big form to join me.

The coven Master stripped off his jeans, stepped to the head of the mattress, and dropped the tip of his long fishing rod into my mouth.

Shifting to sit up, I used both hands on his cock to hold it steady while I sucked as much of it as I could into my mouth. If Master and I were going to put on a show, the Maestro would need his baton in the hardest shape possible.

Golden drops of pre-cum appeared on the slit of his magnificent cock head as I sucked him. These were the next best thing to his cum in order to truly taste my Master's life-force—to know him and experience him. I sucked them down greedily and tried to milk more from his big tool as fast as I could.

Master got hard in a hurry. I could feel that he was ready to fuck and so was I. I had already lubed myself in the cabin before coming out, so we were completely ready to go. Master pulled his cock from my lips and asked me, "Are you ready, Servant?"

"Ready, Master." I had almost forgotten that there were so many people watching because they were so quiet and still. Or maybe it was because I was totally focused on pleasuring my Master. Whichever it was, it didn't matter because I was where I wanted to be.

Atlanta . . .

The big man knelt on the mattress below my ass while I lay back down and lifted my legs away from him. He took my left leg and placed it to the side of his knee on the mattress while he lifted the other way up onto his shoulder. I was glad that I had stretched out my muscles before coming out because this was a new position for us and it was serious. My Master was not playing around.

I desire for us to be in Atlanta . . .

I soon saw Master's logic in this position because it opened up my entire ass to the crowd to see. He wanted them to watch him pound my pud into submission, but at the same time, he wanted them to see the magic happen. Master leaned forward and placed his cock head on my puckered hole. He hesitated as he checked on me one last time.

I made sure to have Atlanta running through my mind as my Master pushed his hips forward and plunged his manhood inside me. It felt like I was a piece of dried wood being felled by an axe—like I was going to be split into two pieces by my big lumberjack.

I want to go to Atlanta. I want to go to Atlanta . . .

Master kept pushing. He slammed his big meat all the way inside me until I was completely full of him and his short hairs were tickling my ass cheeks. My anal ring was stretched to its maximum in the effort to surround his big piece of meat. A murmur went up from the crowd at either his awesome display of power or my ability to take it.

I want us to go to Atlanta . . .

The blue energy ring appeared almost immediately after I opened my eyes. I was full of my Master's hot throbbing cock and in response the blue energy ring became brighter and more pronounced than I ever remember it being. It beautifully lit up the campsite around us with its smoky blue aura.

I want to go to Atlanta . . .

I felt some kind of connection to the energy. Maybe that was just the knowledge that Master and I had discovered that the energy ring could read our desires and fulfill them. It was hard not to feel a part of something that granted your wishes.

Go to Atlanta . . .

The criminals were frightened at first, based on the sounds they were making and the comments they were saying to each other. I could not concentrate on them when I had my man on top of me. He was insistent and commanding—a figure larger than life that demanded all of me not just my body, but my mind and my attention also.

To Atlanta . . .

"Gage," he whispered to me as his body completed a perfect ninety-degree angle with my ass.

"Master, I am yours. Destroy me."

Atlanta. Atlanta . . .

There were no more exchanges of words between us as Master started to fuck me. He held my leg straight up from my ass into the air and with each of his thrusts, his sweaty hairy chest and body formed to it like we were molded together. It was an impressive fuck—his cock delving deep inside me and my ass muscles clenching his big rod for dear life. It was a fuck for the record books and we both needed it.

Atlanta . . .

The blue energy ring pulsed in time with Master's thrusts. It started to contract and expand, getting larger and larger each time. The blue smoke stretched further and further into the crowd and then into the forest before coming back to center on Master and myself. Amazingly, it also felt like Master's throbbing cock was also expanding with each thrust. It felt like I had a bomb buried deep inside me that was about to explode. He held onto my arms to keep his thrusts from sending me across the mattress.

Lanta . . .

I could no longer hear the mutterings of the crowd, because the buzzing of the blue energy ring was suddenly very pronounced in my ears. Master was pumping his cock into me like he had just been released from a cage himself. We were both sweating profusely and my ass was burning just like he had set it aflame.

Suddenly, I felt my body vibrating. Not just shaking, but every muscle in my body vibrating back and forth. It was as if some god had taken a tuning fork and held it up to each one of my muscles at the same time. My teeth started to chatter until I closed them tight and held them there. Having my Master fuck me with such speed and power while having all of my muscles vibrate out of control was too much stimulation for me. My body reacted the only way it knew how to release the pressure.

Ta . . .

My cock filled with blood to its absolute limit and then my balls released the signal that I was going to cum. My back arched and I could feel that my Master was right with me. I looked up into his dark eyes and knew we were on the same plane.

Suddenly the blue energy circle closed in on us and outlined the forms of our fucking bodies perfectly. I could only feel it like a tingle on my skin. Selfishly, I didn't want Master to stop drilling me even though something amazing was happening. The blue ring melded with our skins and I lost my sight, as well as all of my senses.

A second later, I could feel again and I was lying on something hard. Master was above me fucking down into me like his life depended on it. The blue smoke from the energy ring swirled around us, but I saw no signs of the energy now.

I reached down and held up the base of my painful cock. Master thrust deep inside me one last time before pulling his powerful dick out of me and holding it above my chest like the end of a garden hose watering a dry plant. He finally released my leg and I lowered it for even more sensations.

Master and I both came in magnificent explosions. Hot white cum rained down on my face, neck, and chest. I opened my mouth to try to harvest as much of my Master's life-force as I could. He spewed over me creating a white rainbow of his essence. We were both breathing hard and sweating like pigs as we finished.

Suddenly, there was thunderous applause to my left and both Master and I looked toward it. I could see that we were in a theater of some sort and it was packed full of people who were all clapping and cheering for us.

What the fuck?

CHAPTER EIGHTEEN

Part of a text string between two friends on that same night.

Kevin, man did you miss a show tonight!

Why? Where did you go?

Remember that kinda odd guy that I work out with sometimes at the gym that I was telling you about?

Yeah, Rob?

That's him. We went out to grab something to eat last week and he told me something odd.

What?

He told me that he was a warlock.

Like a witch?

Yeah. He was real serious about it and I didn't really believe it, so he did some crazy shit with the food on my plate.

Like what?

Changed it different colors, changed it into other types of food, made it disappear, shit like that . . .

Maybe he's a magician

Whatever . . . he was pretty fucking slick with it. Anyway, he told me about this club that they have uptown.

There's more than one of them?

I know . . . holy shit, right? He said they were having this big show tonight and that I should come see it.

That's where you were tonight?

That's where I still am. You won't believe this shit that I'm getting ready to tell you . . .

This place is like a typical bar, but it has a big stage. There was a live band and the booze was flowing. And get this, it was free. I haven't paid for a single beer yet.

No fucking way. Why aren't we there every night?

I know, right? Anyway the band stops and the singer announces that it is time for the first act. He says that the coven Master from some Warlock tribe in Romania is going to put in an appearance.

What was he like?

Big as fucking shit. But the weird thing was that as we watched the stage, this blue smoke shit filled the club and then there was a crack like a thunderbolt. I looked at the stage and that man had appeared out of the smoke and he was fucking this marked dude as hard as he could as they rode on some sort of copper magic carpet . . .

LOL. What kind of drugs did you take before you went? And where can I get some?

Master leaned down to me so that he could be heard over the noise around us and said, "Fantastic show, Gage. We did it."

"Made it to Atlanta, Master?"

"Yes, my Servant. I have two friends that own this club, who I have not seen for a very long time. I asked them if we could pay a visit and they very wisely found a way to capitalize on it," he answered with a smirk. Master lifted up and helped me stand as well. He seemed to be searching the darkened room.

A deep voice called from behind us, "We are here, Roman."

Master and I both turned to look and saw two huge warlocks enter the stage from the split in the curtains. They stepped out onto the middle of the stage and took a bow to more thunderous applause.

The two big men could not have been more different at

first glance, although after I studied them, they probably had a lot in common. They looked like they were both in their early thirties. They were both tall and broad, just like my Master and me.

The first one was a gym rat. He was handsome with dark blond hair that was shaved mostly in a military cut. He wore a colorful tank top that showed off his cut chest and some of the largest fucking biceps that I have ever seen in person. Basketball shorts and tennis shoes finished off his just-from-the-gym look.

The second one was less bodybuilder and looked more like a professional football player—someone who was thick with muscles that were undefined. His black hair was shaved on the sides and back and when he took off his black cowboy hat to take a bow, I saw that his hair was cut short on top in military style also. He had a full black beard and wore a blue suit with black cowboy boots. A hunting knife hung from a pouch on his belt and a burning cigar was between his thick fingers. I noticed that even the backs of his hands and the tops of his fingers were covered in black hair, so I assumed that he was covered everywhere with it.

Neither man was as tall, broad, or muscular as my Master, but then who could be?

The blond guy addressed the crowd. "All right, all right. Settle down. That was just Act One!"

The crowd burst out in an uproar again.

The dark one yelled, "Our friends will be back to show you something else in just a little while. Have a drink and be patient, you bunch of fucks!"

Both men bowed again and then spun around to face us. Almost as if it had been choreographed, both men took long sweeping looks at my Master and focused on his tremendous cock.

The blond one finally spoke. "Roman, you certainly

have . . . grown since your last visit."

Master looked down and said, "That is Dart's influence on me, brother. He makes me a better version of myself."

The black haired one said, "Yes, I can see that." He turned to me, grabbed the front of his crotch through his suit pants, and said, "Maybe the famous Mr. Dart will make my cock even longer and thicker than it is now."

"Maybe you can show us where we might shower," Master said drolly. "Servant, these are two of my oldest friends." He indicated the blond and said, "This is Timber." He pointed at the other one and said, "And the man who wants his dick bigger before he even meets you is Tomcat."

"And your name is Roman, Master?" I asked.

"Nickname, little one. And don't think just because you just put on the performance of a lifetime and gave me a fuck for the centuries that you won't be punished for asking that." His dark eyes blazed at me.

"Yes, Master," I said as I hung my head.

"It was an amazing performance," Timber told us.

"And the fact that you came riding in on this bronze carpet was so cool," Tomcat added.

"That is the top of the mattress that we started fucking on," Master told his two friends.

Both sets of their eyes opened wider. "You did an alchemical spell while you were fucking?"

Master sighed and looked down at me. I took that as my chance to explain. "If Master or I are touching anything natural, like wood, paper, cotton, or plants while we are fucking, they turn into some type of metal," I explained. "It isn't a spell we cast, but a product of our union."

"No fucking way!" Tomcat said. "I can't wait to see what you two do next on this stage."

"We have to go again?" Master asked with disbelief.

Tomcat said, "We promised the crowd." He looked down

at me and said, "But if you don't want to fuck this sweet piece of tail on stage in a half hour, I'm sure that I could arrange for someone else to do it."

Master bristled and said, "I have no problems fucking Dart anywhere I want, whenever I want, but I am nobody's puppet."

"They just want to see the magic," Timber said.

"And so do we," Tomcat added after taking a big puff from his cigar. "If it is everything that Roman has told us it is, then we will be in awe of your magic again."

"We shall show them, right, Dart?"

"Yes, Master."

Timber took me by the arm, propelled me forward behind the curtain, and said, "You will probably want to soak in a hot bath back here until it is time to go again. I don't even know how you were able to take that big monster he has swinging between his legs before you puffed him up, but now — Regardless, we will fix you right up."

He escorted me to a room beneath the stage which contained a soaking tub already full of hot water. I didn't hesitate to get into it, wincing at the pain of lifting my legs over the rim.

"God, he fucked you hard, didn't he?" Timber asked. He waved his hand over the water and produced bath salts that rained down from his palm into the water.

"You know him better than I do. What do you think?"

Timber laughed and said, "I think Roman has finally found someone who can handle his lust."

"Roman has done what?" My Master's voice boomed in the small ceilinged room. He was wearing an over-sized robe when he moved into my field of vision.

Timber turned and said, "I've never seen you fuck like that before, Roman. Not that I didn't think you could, but you never had a partner who could keep up with you."

"Dart certainly has been able to keep up with me," Master said, his gaze focusing right on me.

"Fuck! We're going to have a great show!" Tomcat said excitedly.

"If you two could give us a moment, I would appreciate it. I need to speak to my Servant for a few minutes."

"Sure. Anything," Timber said as he opened the door to leave. "I'll knock when you have five minutes."

Master knelt carefully beside the tub and asked, "I didn't hurt you, did I, Gage?"

"No, Master. I always want you to fuck me that hard and deep, but afterward I'm going to be wreaked for a while."

"I know you want to go see your father and I promise we will tomorrow. I just need to do one last experiment with you to satisfy my curiosity, and since Tim and Tom live so close to your dad, I couldn't pass up the opportunity."

"No problem, Master. I have every confidence in you."

"If I asked you to fuck with my two friends, would you hate it?"

"No, Master. They are both hot little versions of you."

He snorted and said, "They are my cousins."

Suddenly it hit me why Master was asking this of me. "You want to see if the magic between us happens with someone else of your bloodline, Master?"

"You are just as smart as desirable, little one. Yes, I want to see if that makes a difference."

I looked at him thoughtfully. "Did they change physically like you and I did when we met, Master?"

"No, but we didn't change either until after we fucked. So, I wonder if I am messing with the parameters of the spell's magic. I will go away tomorrow and let them enjoy you. You will report back to me as we go see your father. Understand, little one?"

"Yes, Master." I was skeptical that this experiment would

wind up producing anything other than another sore asshole for me to deal with, but who was I to complain? I had not felt the buzzing in my head or the vibration in my body that I had felt when my Master was near me the first time either.

"You want to shower in here, Master?" I finally asked him.

"Do you mind me sweaty and smelling like cum?" he asked with a raised eyebrow.

I chuckled and said, "Absolutely not, my Master."

"I didn't think so. You soak, Gage. I'm going to catch up with my friends. I will be back to get you. Do not leave this room."

"Yes, sir."

I watched my big guy exit the room before putting my head back and closing my eyes. I'm not sure how long I had them closed when I heard a sound in the room.

Opening my eyes and turning toward the noise, I saw someone in the room with me. I didn't recognize him. "Who the fuck are you?" I challenged.

"I'm no one. I just want to know what kind of magic you perform."

I looked at the skinny man who looked like a teenager. His hair looked greasy and not taken care of. His clothes were all black and thread-bare but looked clean enough.

"What?" I asked, stalling for time. I stood up and wrapped a nearby towel around my waist. If I was going to fight, I wanted to be ready.

"The magic. I don't recognize it." He held up his palm and produced a ball of fire. "I'm quite accomplished, but I do not know the type of magic that you do. I would like to know," he admitted.

I was stumbling for an answer when the door opened and my Master and his two friends walked in laughing. He saw me standing in the tub with the look of uncertainty on my face and immediately went into protect mode.

He whirled on the teen who had invaded my privacy. Master was on him in a heartbeat. The stranger's back was soon up against the wall as my Master held him there by the throat.

"What are you doing in here?" my Master growled.

"It's Larry," Timber said. "He hangs around the bar all the time, trying to suck all the magic out of everyone."

My Master lowered Larry to the ground and stepped away from him but kept his big body between me and the stranger.

Tomcat raised his voice and said, "Larry, you know that you are not allowed back here. Didn't we have this conversation before?"

Larry looked nervous and said, "I must know what this magic is that these two do."

"You'll leave now on your own volition or in a few seconds by stretcher," my Master growled.

Larry reached inside his jacket and pulled a very sharp-looking wavy knife from an inside pocket. He had a very odd look on his face that made him appear to be deranged.

Master took one step toward the teenager and suddenly I feared for his safety. At the same time, a horrible pain came from my lower back causing me to arch and stiffen. I felt my feet leave the bottom of the tub just as I noticed that the golden glow was back. I was rising out of the tub. Looking down in a panic, I saw that two golden branches had sprouted from my Master's glyph on my lower back.

One branch was holding back my Master and the other one had entwined Larry and made him drop the knife. I didn't know how I was doing it or even if I was doing anything at all. All I knew was that my Master was safe now.

With that realization, the golden light started to dim, I slowly returned to the tub from mid-air, and the golden branches receded into the dark mark on my lower back. Tomcat and Timber just looked at me with wide eyes and open mouths. Master leapt at Larry and held him tightly just like he was the honeysuckle branches.

"What the fuck is he?" Timber asked, still staring wide-eyed at me.

"I need your magic," Larry said in awe.

I looked at my Master to see if he thought I was some kind of freak or not. He looked at me with such desire that I knew instantly that we were okay.

"What was in your mind at that moment, Dart?" he asked. His voice was husky with desire.

"I was fearful that you would be hurt, Master," I admitted.

"Your instinct was to protect me."

"Yes, Master."

He smiled and said, "I appreciate that, little one." He handed Larry over to Tomcat who promised to throw him out of the club and ban him for life.

Master came over to me and gave me a giant bear hug.

"You don't think I am a freak, Master?"

"No, Dart. I don't know what you are, but it doesn't matter to me. You want to protect me and satisfy my desires. I want you more than ever."

I felt A huge weight lifted off of my soul and I hugged him back.

"Whatever you two are getting ready to do, let's do it up on the stage," Timber said, like a true entrepreneur.

"I don't know why we have to perform in your dog and pony show," Master grumbled.

"Tit for tat," Timber said. "If you want us to be part of your little experiment—"

"Like you would pass up the opportunity to fuck this fine piece of ass," Master said while grabbing my naked buns and turning them toward his friend.

Timber chuckled and admitted, "It probably wouldn't be much of a stand-off while you are holding the trump card."

"Damn straight," Master said. "Let's go, little one. We will put on a show, get some sleep, conduct our experiment in the morning, and then go see Papa Dart."

"I'm ready, Master." I followed both men out onto the stage where a mattress had been laid out for us.

Timber faced the drinking crowd, raised his voice, and asked, "Has anyone brought any herbs with them tonight?"

Two men shouted that they had, so Timber brought them up onto the stage and introduced them to us. One of them gave Timber a handful of mint and the other several sprigs of thyme.

The two men left the stage. Timber turned to us and asked if there was anything else. Master looked down at me.

"Is there anything in your club that you want updated, Timber?" I asked.

"We were going to paint and change the lights at the end of the season," he said.

"What color?" I asked.

"We want it red with black accents."

I looked at Master who nodded his head at me.

Timber caught on immediately and turned back to the crowd. "Not only are these two going to transform these herbs which each man can testify are true plants into something else, but they are also going to help us redecorate the club tonight."

The crowd cheered and Master lay down on the mattress with his head toward the back curtain. He spread his massive legs and I dropped between them to suck on his magnificent organ. He was already mostly hard, as usual, and leaking pre-cum, so I set right about to swallowing as much of that as possible.

When Master was hard as a fucking I-beam, I held his cock up for the crowd to see. There was a murmur that ran through the crowd and then applause. I took the time to lube myself and also my Master before I climbed into the saddle.

Hovering pretty far above Master's crotch, I placed the giant cock head of the dick I loved more than any other on my puckered hole. Slowly, I let gravity pull me down until his cock head had popped inside me. Closing my eyes, I willed my anal ring to expand around his throbbing member as it plunged deeper and deeper inside me.

Master's hands were on my ass cheeks, spreading them apart. Once I was sitting on his crotch, he spread his legs, bent his knees, and placed his feet on the mattress so that all in attendance could see his cock splitting my asshole in half.

"You are mine," Master grunted.

"I am yours."

The blue energy ring appeared as soon as he thrust his hips forward and I was completely impaled on his cock. I belonged to this man and I didn't care who knew it.

CHAPTER NINETEEN

Part of a journal entry in the Trad Grimoud written by the Coven Master the next day, the fourteenth of April, 2019.

My servant's powers grow with each day.

Yesterday he thought I was in danger and became extremely concerned for my safety. This level of high energy brought out new magic in him that I was unaware he possessed.

I had previously marked him with a glyph — the honeysuckle bush which is my sigil. The magic used to make the mark was also a piece of unusual magic produced by our coupling. In this time of great stress, his psychic mark became real and sought to protect me.

A warlock with a knife was threatening us and Gage rose into the air. His glyph began to glow with a golden light and then honeysuckle branches grew from his lower back. The branches entwined the intruder and disabled him before retreating back into my Servant.

Gage is noticeably upset by what has happened — more because he fears that I will not like him as a result of it than his understanding of what the magic is and why. I have tried to relieve his stress, because I am more intrigued with him than ever. This is the first magic I have seen from him that was not done while I was fucking him and that is significant.

After breakfast, we will conduct our experiment here to see if those of my blood can produce the same magic with Gage or not. I do not hold high hopes for a positive result, because all of the signs are not here that were true when I first met my Servant.

Tonight, we travel to meet Gage's father. I am not looking for-

ward to it, because what man wants to see his son become a sex slave to another man. Not to mention that his son has been sold into the sex trade and held captive for the last four years, gets released, and then immediately goes right back to it again. There is no way that this can end well.

I am ready with several spells in case I have to use them. I think the Forgetting Spell would be the most humane one to use and the one that would be least damaging to Gage.

Master and I spent the night at the home of Tomcat and Timber. Their house was large and beautifully furnished. The guest room had a king-sized bed that they told me was just for my Master when he came to visit. I slept hard and woke up to the smell of coffee and bacon.

My Master was already out of bed, so I brushed my teeth and followed the smell of food to the kitchen.

"There he is," Master said happily when he saw me. "Come sit on my lap, little one."

"That is the reason that I cannot sit today, Master." It did not escape my notice that all three of the cousins were shirtless. My Master's dark hairy chest was replicated on Tomcat, only slightly smaller in size. Timber had a shaved chest with gloriously cut pecs to match his magnificent biceps. It was all I could do not to stare.

The three warlocks laughed at my joke.

"Are you refusing me, Servant?" Master asked.

"No, sir. I would never do that, Master."

He chuckled and ordered me to eat. I filled a plate full of eggs, bacon, fried potatoes, and fruit. Master made coffee for me with extra cream while I fixed my plate. I stood at the table while the three giant men sat and talked.

"Jesus, Roman, don't you ever let the boy wear clothes?"

Master turned and looked at my naked body. "Not really. He is a thing of beauty is he not?"

Tomcat laughed and said, "That he is."

"I guess I'll have to have something for him to wear to see his father," Master said while rubbing his bearded chin. "I don't want to rub it in Daddy's face that his only son is constantly at my sexual beck and call."

"There's a new store right around the corner from us that has some nice things, if you want," Timber offered.

Master shook his head and said, "Maybe I'll do that while you guys get busy."

I continued to eat, not wanting to look up. Master was such a turn-on for me and now throwing his two big handsome cousins into the mix, I was barely able to contain myself. I could feel my face heating up already.

"Do you feel safe with my cousins, little one? They are powerful warlocks in their own right."

I looked up from my plate into my Master's dark eyes. "Yes, Master."

"Are you ready to serve them for the next two hours just as you would serve me?"

"Yes, Master."

"You will give them your best, Dart, or you will be severely punished. Do you understand?"

"I do, Master, and I will not disappoint you."

He grabbed me by the scruff of my neck and squeezed. "I know that you will not. Let's go shower together, little one."

I quickly ate the last piece of toast on my plate and thanked the boys for the breakfast before following my Master to the guest bath.

He had dropped his basketball shorts as soon as he was inside the bathroom. I waited while he adjusted the water temperature before I followed him into the shower.

"You may scrub me clean, Servant," his deep voice boomed in the glass rectangle of the shower.

Gladly, Master . . .

Grabbing a loofah and some body wash, I was soon

scrubbing the glorious body that I worshipped more than any other in the world. Selfishly, I took my time, making sure Master was clean.

"What do you think your father's reaction will be tonight, Gage?" Master asked softly.

"He will be relieved, Master. He will be happy to see me." I continued to scrub his thick legs.

"Yes."

"He will want to know everything that has happened to me, Master," I said quietly. I scrubbed his beautiful hairy ass cheeks.

"And will you tell him?"

"I think so. It is his right to know." I concentrated on scrubbing his lower back, massaging more than cleaning.

"Are you worried about his reaction to me at all?" he asked carefully.

I moved on to covering his broad back with the bubbles coming from the loofah. "I am, Master."

A large breath escaped from Master's lips. "So am I, little one." He spun around to face me.

"What do you expect, Master?" I asked suddenly looking up into his face.

"There could be police involvement," he answered. "Or your father may take out his anger on me."

"That doesn't sound like him," I said as I started to scrub his massive chest. "The police, maybe. I could see that, but my dad is not violent. He will not blame you for this."

"It is a lot for him to deal with—the abduction, your abuse, your imprisonment, the long four years of worry, not to mention that you were saved by a warlock who is now your Master."

"He will see that you are my world and he will not interfere with that," I said as I dropped to my knees. I engorged myself on his hard tool as I pulled down on his massive ball sack.

I will not let him . . .

Master put his hand on my head and said, "You are my world also, Gage. You are unlike anyone I have ever met before."

Ditto, Master . . .

I gave my Master a blow job for the ages and he came with a tremendous discharge that choked me. I cleaned us both before we left the shower and dried us with really fluffy towels that made me ask Master if we could get some like them for his cabin.

Master and I joined his cousins in the workout room they had installed in their house. They were both lifting weights and had already developed a sheen of sweat on their skins.

"Trying to pump your selves up for Dart?" Master asked them.

"Getting our reps in while we are waiting to fuck that sweet ass," Tomcat said.

"You leaving for the store?" Timber asked.

"Yeah. You guys enjoy Dart and we will gather the results when I get back."

"We flipped for who was first," Timber said. "I won," he added with a huge grin at his brother. "Want me to shower, Dart?"

"Absolutely not," I answered. I loved a sweaty man. I had already noticed that neither of Master's cousins had an elemental smell like the other warlocks, so musky man would have to do to turn me on.

I looked at my Master and asked, "Is he going to let me boss him around, Master?"

Master looked at his cousin and said, "You have to master him, Tim. You can't care whether he wants you sweaty or not. You just do it whichever way you want. In order for the experiment to be as accurate as possible, you have to become his Master."

"Okay, okay. I just don't have any experience with that."

"Neither did I," Master said.

"He was just a natural at it," I added, which promptly received a glare from my Master and then a chuckle.

"You at least have had your coven to order around," Timber said.

"And you, your employees," Master reminded him.

"All right," Timber relented, changing his voice to a deeper one. "Dart, get your ass in my bed or you will be punished."

"Yes, sir!" I said as I left the workout room in search of Timber's bedroom. I already missed my Master, but I was sure that his cousins would keep me busy until he returned.

I finally located both bedrooms, but was unsure of which one belonged to which brother, so I waited in the hallway in The Service Squat. The squat always drove NOMARs out of their minds. It was a full crouch—up on your toes, with your thighs spread wide open, your forearms on top of your thighs, and your head bowed. It was completely a subservient position and one that every marked man was supposed to be in when in the presence of his Master. I was fortunate that the man who was my true Master did not require me to drop down into the squat every time I was in his presence.

I looked up when I heard Timber coming. He pointed at the right door and I scrambled inside onto the unmade bed. He was just wearing pajama pants, which completely showed off his fabulous body. Once the door was closed, he dropped his pants revealing a big thick dirk between his legs. I had learned from the warlocks that a dirk was a long-thrusting dagger that they used in many spells and I certainly hoped that Timber knew how to use it on me.

"Suck my cock," he ordered.

"Yes, sir," I said as I scrambled off the bed and onto the floor at his feet.

I lifted his cock and felt its substantial heft before plunging my mouth over it. His skin was hot to the touch and had the salty taste of sweat. Timber's cock was one long piece of meat—the head was the exact size of the shaft without much delineation between the two. The base was the also the same size, making his cock one long thick sausage.

Timber got hard in a few seconds and was ready to fuck. I had not felt anything magical or unusual while I was sucking on his fat rod. It felt like any other dick that I had ever sucked, except for the size of course, but it was not special like the one that hung between my Master's legs.

"Up on the bed. Let me see what you have between those cute little ass cheeks."

I spit out his cock and got onto all fours on the bed. Timber spread my ass cheeks with his hands and spit on my puckered hole. He rubbed his finger over it, giving me chills before he plunged one of them inside me.

"Doesn't seem big enough to take me. How in the hell do you take that big Roman column he has now?"

"It is very flexible, sir."

"It better be," he said as he went to the nightstand and got a tube of lube. He spread some on my hole before pounding his cock with a greased palm.

"You know, Dart, I've never seen your Master like this before."

"Like what, sir?"

"I've never seen him care for someone like he does you. Maybe that is because he has never really had someone he was close to before. He usually does not let anyone inside, you know?"

"He is my everything," I admitted.

"I can tell. He has not only opened up to you, but you have brought out something in him that we have never seen."

"Master has a lot to offer the world," I said confidently.

"I have a lot to offer you," he growled as he pushed his hips forward and guided his cock into my backside.

I hung my head and tried to relax as Timber tore a hole through my anal ring. He was not as thick or long as my Master, but he was still a difficult dick to take.

"Aw, fuck! That's a tight hole squeezing my cock. I just assumed after Roman has been fucking you for so long that you would be a stretched-out mess, but man, I was wrong."

"I am to please."

"No wonder Roman is infatuated with you." Timber was holding himself above me, waiting for me to get used to his cock being inside me.

"He's hardly infatuated. He's my Master and he has to think about and plan for both of us," I said defensively. I made a mental note that there was no blue energy ring that emanated from us.

"Okay, whatever you say. But I'm telling you that he is a different man with you. It is amazing to see."

"What would be amazing to see would be you giving me a hard, deep fuck. Do you think you can handle that?"

"I can handle that all right. I was just waiting for the blue energy ring."

"It would have already come by now," I said to him with a face that indicated that I realized he was disappointed.

I was not disappointed. I wanted what Master and I had to be just for us. That made it more special in my mind.

"Alrighty then!" he said before beginning to pump his ass up and down.

It was a good fuck. Timber was a good man. But he was not in the same league as my Master.

CHAPTER TWENTY

Part of a message from Gage, the coven Master's Servant, written to his father and delivered by text from Timber's cellphone on the morning of April fourteenth, 2019.

Dad,

I cannot believe how technology has advanced the four years that I have been away.

Texting is so foreign to me, but my friends assure me that is the best way to contact you without actually speaking to you.

We are in Atlanta and will leave tonight to come see you.

We should be there by dinner time.

My Master will accompany me, because he doesn't trust anyone with my security except himself.

I have a feeling that you will like him, if not for his personality, at least for the fact that he rescued me and continues to keep me safe.

It feels good to be back in the US again and Atlanta makes me miss the South and you even more.

I can't wait to see you.

I'm hoping you haven't changed very much.

I'm afraid that I have and I hope that you will recognize me.

I'm fearful of a lot of things, but I guess I have to keep going forward . . .

"You don't need to fuck him, Tomcat. I just did and while there were major fireworks, there is no magic. So, you are not needed," Timber told his brother when the two of us found him still in the weight room. I was impressed that Tomcat had been working out for that long.

"Like fuck, I don't," Tomcat spit as he performed another bicep curl which beautifully outlined his big muscle. He was sweaty from head to toe. His clothing was soaked through.

Timber laughed and said, "He's all yours."

"How was he?" Tomcat asked as he performed another curl. He was clearly talking to his brother but looked at me with the eyes of a wolf in front of a juicy rabbit.

"You don't have to talk about me like I'm not even in the room," I said sarcastically.

"Fabulous," Timber said, ignoring me. "You'll see why Roman is all about him."

"Awesome," Tomcat said as he sat back on the machine. He awkwardly pushed his gym shorts onto his legs, looked at me, and asked, "You think you are something because you are the first Servant that Roman has ever had?"

"No, I think I am something because I am," I told him with an even tone to my voice. "Your cousin sees that in me and because he thinks so, he has made me his Servant."

Tomcat laughed but did not stop his workout. "You certainly are confident in yourself."

"Would your cousin like me to be any other way?" I asked him with a smirking face.

Tomcat laughed and I heard Timber chuckle beside me also. "No, no, he wouldn't."

"I didn't think so," I said, borrowing one of my Master's favorite lines when dealing with me.

Tomcat finally looked up and ordered, "Get over here and show your Master's cousin why you are the one, Dart."

"Yes, sir," I said as I made my way through the equipment to him. Tomcat was physically like the smaller version of my Master, so I couldn't wait to get my tongue on those sweaty hairy muscles of his.

It didn't escape my notice that Tomcat continued to perform bicep curls even as I swallowed his fat cock. My head was buried in his sweaty crotch before I started to pump up and down on him. His dick didn't take long to harden to its limit, so I was soon bent over a cross bar with Tomcat fucking me from behind.

"How many times did my brother fuck you?" he asked in between thrusts into my sore ass.

"Twice," I answered, trying to hold onto the slippery metal bar against my chest.

"Then I shall go three," he announced.

"Go ahead, stud," I encouraged him.

"I can see why Roman has a thing for you," he said. "Your mouth is just average, but your hole is really transcendent."

"Thanks, Tomcat," I said with more than a little bite. "I'm surprised such a meathead as you even knows the word transcendent."

He chuckled and said, "That average mouth has some bite, I guess. So far the sex is awesome, but nothing magical is happening for me."

"Doesn't seem that way," I said, agreeing with him.

Tomcat did live up to besting his brother that day, but even with the relentless pounding I had received, I had not cum. My dick was hard but not painfully so like it was with my Master, and there had been no magical sparks, even when Tomcat folded me in half on top of the weight bench and fucked down into me, looking like a giant black bear.

I spent the next hour soaking in a hot bath until my Master arrived. He sat down on the edge of the tub and tousled my wet hair.

"I heard there were no fireworks," he said evenly.

"Not even a spark, Master."

"And do you think that you gave them your very best, little one?" he asked with one raised eyebrow that was so cute I wanted to climb out of the bathtub and mount him right there.

"I tried, Master."

"You must have succeeded, Gage. Neither one of them can stop talking about you and how they have never felt an ass like yours before," Master said while smirking.

I blushed furiously under his intent dark stare.

"Do you have any ideas why there was not any magic between the three of you?"

I looked him right in the eyes and said, "It is just for you, Master. You and I are the keys to the magic."

"You are probably right, little one."

"I am very fortunate to have been saved by you, my Master," I told him in all seriousness.

"I was very lucky to have claimed you, my Servant."

I smiled up at the big man who my world revolved around. He was so stinking hot that my dick began to harden immediately.

"Are you ready to go see your father? I have rented a car," he told me with a small grin on his face.

"Yes, Master!" I answered excitedly. "A car?" I asked with surprise in my voice.

"Yes, Gage, a car."

"Not a motorcycle?"

"I prefer them of course, but I want to carefully craft the first image of me that your father is going to have and a car is much more respectable, is it not?" he asked me, eyes blazing.

"It is, but is it necessary, Master?" The man known by his cousins as Roman was just as smart and cunning as I considered myself and that was a very attractive feature to his character.

"We can't very well fuck and teleport there or the first

image your father will have of you is riding my pole. And while that is a glorious image to me, I don't think he would appreciate it."

I blushed and said, "Oh, I thought you could just send us by clapping your hands together like you did the warlocks at the compass round during the black moon."

"Yes, we can do that. It is so much faster than actually driving, but we will need the car to complete the illusion."

I nodded when I understood.

"Get dressed and let's say goodbye to our friends," he commanded as he stood up from the edge of the tub.

I was momentarily stunned by what he was saying and by what he was wearing. "Get dressed?"

"Yes, your Master is saying to put on clothes for the first time ever. Don't get used to it," he smirked. "And I will not forget that you just failed to use my title and that you have questioned my decisions. I will have to punish you later for both of those infractions."

"Yes, Master," I agreed. The thought of Master punishing me made me even more excited than I already was, but at the same time brought a feeling of dread into my heart. What if he wanted to fuck someone else again like he had during my last punishment? I was so jealous of anyone being with my Master that the image in my head made me want to go postal.

My heightened state of horniness was not helped by the sight in front of me either. I was almost openly panting at the outfit that my Master had picked out to wear to meet my father. He was dressed in a black t-shirt that clung to every gigantic muscle of his upper body. Army fatigues and black boots completed the look with a green webbed belt to offset his smaller waist. He looked like an army commando that was ready to storm a beach.

"I see that you approve of my outfit, little one," he said

with a smile as he tweaked my hard cock.

"It's perfect for army maneuvers or for making me hard as a fucking rock, Master, but do you want to give my father the impression that you are in the military?"

"I want him to see that I have discipline and that I will keep his son safe. That is the impression that I want him to have of me."

"And it does that," I said while nodding my head.

"Let's go see Papa Gage," he said, changing my mood immediately.

"Yes, sir!" I quickly dried off and put on some of the new clothes that Master had bought for me.

He had purchased several tee shirts, a pair of jeans, several pair of board shorts, tennis shoes, flip flops, socks, a belt and a dress shirt. He had even bought us two small suitcases to carry everything inside.

"No underwear, Master?" I asked as I continued to look through the bags.

"No Servant of mine will ever wear underwear, little one. You will be ready for me to fuck you at a second's notice."

"Yes, Master." I looked at him and wondered if he knew what effects his words had on me or not. I couldn't tell from his poker face, but I did think that I saw him smile as he put a cigar between his teeth and lit it.

I took note from Master's attire and dressed with a little less edge. I chose a red knit Polo shirt and khaki shorts. Sticking my feet into the flip flops he had bought me, I looked in the mirror and decided to do something with my hair. I remembered there was a tube of hair gel in the bathroom on the counter, so I quickly used it, packed up the extra clothes, and indicated to my Master that I was ready to go.

Master turned on heel and I followed him out to the living room. Saying goodbye to Tomcat and Timber, I gave them both big hugs. I was happy to meet some of my Master's family and wanted them to like me. They both wished us well and suggested that we should visit for longer next time.

"You three studs will never let me out of bed, if we come back," I said jokingly.

"Exactly," Tomcat told me with a wink as he walked with us out to the front of the house.

Parked in front of the house was a brand new Jeep Wrangler Rubicon. It was gun-metal grey and shiny with beautiful silver trim.

"That's the car you rented, Master?"

"If I needed to own a car, it would be the one that I would buy," he said with a shrug. "You don't like it, little one?"

"It is hot like my Master," I said simply.

"Don't try to blow smoke up my ass, Dart. I am still going to punish you when I get the chance."

"And that punishment's going to be long and hard," Tomcat goaded me with sudden laughter.

"Yes, Master," I said as I opened the Jeep door and threw our bag inside.

"Mind if we watch, Roman?" Timber asked.

Watch what?

"Feel free," my Master told him as he stepped through the driver's side door opening.

I opened the passenger side door and closed it behind me. Master cranked the engine and rolled down both of the front windows.

"Come and visit us in Romania when you get the chance," Master told his cousins.

"We will," they both said in unison.

"Dart, I want you to hold onto the frame of the car while you are blowing me."

Blowing you?

"Yes, Master," I said by habit more than any need for it to

be said.

"Do you remember the neighborhood around the house you grew up in, Dart?"

"Yes, sir."

"Good. I want you to remember one of the side streets about a block away from the house. Concentrate on that side street while I work the spell." He proceeded to open the fly of his fatigues and pull out his glorious dick.

"You are going to teleport us, Master?"

"Yes, but I have not seen where we are going to come out, so it is very dangerous. If our connection is what I think it is, then your knowledge of the location and my spell work will get us there safely." He said this with as much confidence as if he was telling me that he was going to punish me later, so there was no way for me to question it even if I wanted to do so.

When I didn't respond, he added, "You doubt our connection, little one?"

"I don't, Master. I believe that as long as your big cock is buried inside me that we are unstoppable."

"I am in agreement there," he said as he waved goodbye to Tomcat and Timber and pushed my head into his crotch.

I held onto the door frame as I impaled my mouth on his beef stick. Looking up for a brief instant, I saw that my Master's head was bowed and he was mouthing the enchantment. His cock tasted so delicious that I almost forgot what we were doing here.

Master's cock was hard as a steel beam, as usual and had already started to produce the golden pre-cum that I loved so much. His honeysuckle smell coupled with his natural musk was a toxin that I could not get out of my system. I slobbered my saliva all over his giant knob, licking the parts that I could not fit into my mouth.

The coven Master suddenly arched his back and his massively muscled arms came together over my head. Master's hands violently made contact with each other and a sonic boom went off in the cabin of the Jeep. The reflection of the lights flashed dark and light on the floor mats.

"Gage," Master called with a husky voice.

I could tell that he was on the verge of coming. There was nothing that this big man could keep his body from telling me and I considered myself an expert at reading it.

I didn't bother to answer back, instead choosing to bare down on him. Thrusting my head up and down, I hollowed out my cheeks trying to suck him dry. His oversized hand appeared on my head and held me down just as his hips thrust forward — driving that amazing piece of manhood further into my throat.

He came in a torrent of hot molten cum that shot with force down my esophagus. I held onto him, breathing through my nose and trying not to panic. I rode the waves of his climax until he finally let my head go and I pulled back, letting my mouth fill with his spunky seed.

"Fuck! I love having you with me, little one," he said excitedly as he smashed his hand down onto the steering wheel.

"I seem to be the lucky one, Master," I said after coming all the way off of his prick and licking the sides of his column of flesh.

"It worked, Gage."

"It did?" I asked as I sat up and looked out of the front window of the Jeep.

We were no longer in the city where we had just been, but instead on a tree-lined road consisting of modest houses and well-kept yards. I recognized it immediately as the same place where I had learned to ride a bike without training wheels, where I had built a fort with my friend Alan, and where the ice cream truck would park each summer of my youth.

It was the exact spot that I had visualized in my mind before I started blowing my Master in the front of that Jeep. Now, all three of us were here—Master, me, and the Jeep.

CHAPTER TWENTY-ONE

Part of an internal memo concerning a missing person's report filed in April by Gage's father from the Chief of Police outside of Charleston, South Carolina to his Captains.

The father of the missing boy, Gage, called the station this morning to report that he is almost positive that his son has been rescued and that he will be coming home tonight.

He told the desk sergeant that the kidnappers have been detained and punished, but he has no idea who they are or where they are. He stated that he just wanted to let us know so that we could close the case. He also said that he would check back with us after his son's homecoming to confirm that everything is all right.

I would like to continue to follow this case and fill in the missing blanks.

Simmons, assign a patrol car to stakeout the house and let us know when the boy shows up and with whom.

Carter, assign a set of detectives to go out to the father's house tonight to interview the boy and gather as much information as possible.

We would like to find the predators and make sure they are in custody. The boy may be brainwashed into telling a story that is not true. He may have to be hospitalized against his will until he can be evaluated and his story checks out.

We should detain anyone he comes with and get his story as well.

Keep me informed of the progress at all times.

Questions can be directed to Kushner who will take lead on this investigation.

"Is this the place you were concentrating on, Gage?" my Master asked me as we sat in the middle of the street in our rented Jeep.

"Yes, Master. I think we need to move out of the middle of the street."

"I agree."

"Go to the stop sign and turn right, Master," I directed.

He followed my directions without even a smirk or a promise of punishment. I could feel that he was nervous.

We were now on the street where I had lived as a child. My heart began to race and I looked ahead to see if I could see the top of the roofline. Master was driving slowly.

"It's the grey one on the right with the tree that has been split in half in the front yard, Master."

The sudden focus of his gaze told me right away that he had spotted it and was analyzing every detail of the place. I looked at my old house fondly, remembering things that had happened when I was young and noticing new things about it since I had been gone.

Master pulled right in front of the house instead of into the driveway. He looked over at me and said, "In case we need an emergency departure." He turned off the engine.

"Smart, Master, but I don't think we will."

"Your sense of calm is helping me not be so on edge, Gage," the big man admitted.

"It is hard for me to be calm in your presence, Master, but I am trying."

"I will fuck you long and hard tonight, never once letting you off my dick, not even to sleep. So, you think about that while you are in there." His dark eyes penetrated my very soul.

"You want my cock to be hard as a rock while I am visiting with my father, Master?" I asked with a huge grin.

"Yes. I want it hard in my presence at all times, little one."

"So it shall be, Master." I opened my door and stepped out.

Immediately the front door of the house opened and I saw my father through the screen door. He hesitated at first and then I saw the look on his face when he knew it was me. Opening the screen door, he ran out of the house, across the front porch, and down the stairs to me. I only had time to make it halfway to the house before he had enveloped me in his arms.

"Gage, Gage, Gage," he whispered into my chest. I was much taller now and he looked much older to me.

"Dad, it's me," I said softly over and over to him.

Dad was finally able to pull himself back, but he kept ahold of me with both hands as if I might disappear again. We studied each other's faces—mine hardened by age and situation, his wet with tears with a sunken, hollow look to it.

"You're here," he finally said with a smile.

"I'm here. It's really me," I said, returning his smile. I indicated the hulking figure behind me and said, "Dad, this is my Master, Roman."

"You're the one that saved my boy?" Dad asked as he looked up into the giant warlock's face.

"My trad saved him," Master said, not wanting to take credit for something he actually had not done.

"He arranged the whole operation that saved me, Dad," I told my father. "He is a great leader."

Master went to shake my father's hand, but Dad wrapped him in a big bear hug instead. "Thank you, thank you," my father sobbed.

"It was my pleasure," Master said while mouthing the word *literally* over the head of my father to me.

I couldn't help but giggle. My father let go of Master and

welcomed him to his home. Dad put his arm around my waist and started walking me up to the house.

We walked into the small house that I grew up in and it was exactly as I had left it. I didn't think one thing had changed, except my father's recliner now had a twin.

"Have a seat, have a seat," Dad said nervously. "Can I get you anything to drink?"

We both declined although I would have loved a good stiff shot of brandy or something. My Master looked hulking and out of place in my childhood home.

"Gage, I want to hear everything that happened to you, but first I have some bad news to tell you."

I perked up, sitting on the edge of the couch where Master and I were resting. "What, Dad?"

"Your grandfather has passed, Gage," he told me bluntly.

Master's hand immediately slid down off the back of the couch onto my back. I felt the electric sparks before the warming heat of his contact.

"I thought he might have," I admitted. "Are you handling it okay, Dad?" My father and his father had been very close.

"Better than I could have imagined. I mean it was devastating to lose you and then horrific to lose him right after."

"I'm so sorry," I told him as I stood up and gave him another big hug.

"My second news is better," he said as we both sat back down.

"That's good," I said with a sigh of relief.

My father let out a big breath and asked, "Do you remember Granddad's friend, Ernst?"

"Sure," I admitted. My grandfather and Ernst were best friends—inseparable.

"Well, Ernst had a small stroke right after your Granddad passed, so I took him home from the hospital to look after him for a little while. You know that he never had kids, so he didn't have anyone. We got along so well, that he has never left."

"Oh, so he lives with you now?" I asked, looking toward the stairs.

"Yes, he's out with some buddies, but I'm expecting him back any minute, so that's why I wanted to tell you now."

"I'm glad that you have someone to hang with and I'm glad that Grandpa Ernst has someone to look after him, Dad," I said.

"I didn't do such a good job of looking after you though, did I?" he asked with tears forming in his eyes.

"Stop it," I commanded. I used my authoritarian voice that I had learned from my Master. It drew an instant sharp gaze from him. "What happened to me was entirely my fault, as well as a few bad men who are currently being punished."

"I'm so sorry," my father said.

"No need to be. So, Grandpa Ernst has fully recovered then?" I asked, desperately trying to change the subject.

"He walks with a cane, but mostly recovered."

"You tell me," an older voice said from the doorway.

I looked up and saw the face of my Grandfather's best friend. Leaping off the couch, I ran to him and gave him a hug. He smelled the same and it brought me way back to four years ago in a heartbeat.

"Gage, we are so happy to see you!" he said as he hugged me with his free hand.

"I'm so happy that you are here with Dad," I told him as I separated from him. Noticing that Master had stood up, I started my introduction, "Grandpa Ernst, I would like you to meet the man who rescued me. This is . . ."

I never got to finish my sentence. Grandpa Ernst immediately addressed Master in Witchspeak.

"You are warlock," Ernst said firmly.

My Master answered him back in the same language, "I am and so are you." Both men were sizing each other up, but I was the one flabbergasted. At least I understood what was going on. Based on my father's face, he had no clue what was happening.

"You have enchanted Gage?" Ernest asked Master.

Before my Master could answer, I did so for him, saying in Witchspeak, "Grandpa Ernest, I am enchanted with the man, but not because he has put a spell on me."

Now it was time for my grandfather's best friend to be shocked. He looked at me until his face turned to one of delight and he asked, "Gage, my boy, you are a warlock also?"

"Not really," I answered. When I saw his face of disbelief, I added, "It is really complicated. I guess we need to talk."

"But you speak Witchspeak," Ernest said in protest. "Only warlocks know that language."

"Gage is something . . . else," Master explained to the old man.

Grandpa Ernest stared at me for a few seconds before resuming talking to my Master. "He is bound to you. You have claimed him." It was a statement, not a question.

"I have. He wears my mark on his lower back," Master said unapologetically.

"Let's let Dad into the conversation and then we can talk," I said.

"He doesn't know?" Ernest asked with surprise again.

"I don't think so," I admitted, looking at my father's stunned facial expression.

"Careful," Master warned me.

I switched to English and said, "Dad, I have a lot to tell you. I'm going to need you to sit down."

"I'm going to need a drink, aren't I?" he asked as he sat back down in his favorite recliner.

"Maybe more than one," Master told him. "I'll get some

glasses."

"I've got a snort for all of us," Ernst said, producing a bottle out of the inside pocket of his jacket.

"Ernst!" Dad said when he saw the bottle. "Your doctors told you to give that up."

"What do they know?" he asked as he handed the bottle to my Master who was back with four glasses.

I shot Master a look when I did not recognize the glasses as ones that my father would have in his house. He shrugged his big shoulders and smirked at me. He sat the glasses down on the coffee table and poured a shot of the brown liquid into each one before handing them out.

The four of us each threw our heads back and shot the whiskey. It made my throat burn which reminded me of my Master's scalding load that I had just swallowed, so my cock responded in kind.

Master looked at me, looked at my crotch, and narrowed his eyes at me. I gave him a shrug and a smirk of my own. He mouthed the word *punishment* to me, which did nothing to alleviate my condition.

I put my glass down and pulled a chair over closer to my father's recliner. Sitting down, I put my hand on his shoulder and looked into his eyes. "Dad, I was in a terrible place in Russia and two men came to rescue me. They had powers and could do magic, but they only use them for good."

I let that sink in for a minute before continuing. "It was hard for me to believe also, but I saw what they could do and instead of being scared, I was happy for them and for myself because of what I had gained from it."

Master made me pause by filling up Dad's glass again. My father took another quick shot.

I continued, saying, "These two men were nice and treated me with respect. They took me back to their camp where I started to suffer some physical distress. I wasn't sure what it was—like a buzzing in my head and my whole body rang with energy."

Suddenly Grandpa Ernest had perked up. He turned to my Master and asked, "Did you experience the same discomfort?"

Master looked at him evenly and answered, "Yes."

Ernest continued, "And did the discomfort increase when you were together?"

"It did," Master answered. His eyes suddenly narrowed at the old man as he scrutinized him more thoroughly.

"And did the discomfort stop when you had sex for the first time?"

I immediately blushed in front of my father's gaze, but Master answered with no emotion that it had.

Grandpa Ernest looked very pleased, turned to me, and said, "Continue, Gage."

"When Master stepped into the campsite, I could tell immediately that we were connected, Dad," I told him. "I knew that there was something between us and that it was more than just a sexual attraction."

"The first sign that we had this connection was the way we were drawn to each other," Master told my father.

"You thought he was wearing a talisman?" Ernest asked.

"A very strong one, yes."

I explained to Dad, saying, "Master thought I had done a spell to draw him to me, but I was being drawn to him by the same force that was drawing him to me."

Dad nodded that he understood.

"The second part of our connection was that Master and his gang were speaking a language called Witchspeak which can only be understood by his kind. But I could clearly understand them and could speak it."

"By his kind?" my father asked before taking another shot of whiskey and cutting his eyes at my Master. "What is he?"

I decided to rip the bandage right off, so to speak. "My Master is a warlock."

"A warlock?" he asked, sitting up straighter in his chair. He looked over at Ernest and said, "Gage, did you know that Grandpa was always telling me that he was a warlock?"

Now it was my turn to be shocked. "What?"

"Once he told me years ago when I was a teenager. I didn't believe him, of course, so he did some magic tricks that I spent the next few months trying to figure out how he did them, but I still didn't believe."

"He was an amateur magician," I remembered. "He was always doing some trick for me growing up."

Dad turned to me and looked sad again. "After you were taken, he tried to tell me again, several times. He said that he could do things to help get you back, but I just thought it was his grief manifesting as wishful thinking." Dad's gaze turned back to Ernest.

"Your father was a warlock, Gerald," the old man said evenly.

"But how?" my father asked.

"We were in the same trad together," Ernest said with a kind tone. "When it became evident that you were not going to be magical, he quit the trad to raise you like a normal father."

"You are a warlock also?" Dad asked his new roommate. Dad looked bewildered.

I turned and looked at my Master who nodded to me. This was helping to explain some things for him, I guessed.

"Don't you remember going to our meetings when you were young?" Ernest asked. "You would run around and around the compass round until one of us would put a holding spell on you."

"Those were church meetings. We stopped going to church when I started school . . ."

"Magic was our church," Ernest said kindly.

My Master filled my father's glass with more whiskey.

"So, my father was a warlock, but I'm not."

"That's correct. The magic doesn't always flow from one family member to the next," Ernest told him.

"But now my son is?" Dad asked first Ernest and then my Master.

"I don't think he is a warlock," Master said carefully. "But he definitely has magic in his genes."

Dad looked at me and asked, "You can do magic, Gage?"

"Well, that's just it, Dad. I've never been able to, that I know of, but my Master and I seem to be able to do things when we are . . . together," I said awkwardly.

"Like what?"

I turned to my Master and held my hand up in the air. He understood what I wanted and lifted his hand to mine. Immediately the blue energy crackled and popped in the small space between our palms.

"When does the most magic occur? Is it when you are fucking?" Ernest asked exactly what I was trying not to say.

"Yes," I sighed.

"Spells that you should not be able to perform normally?" Ernest asked Master.

"Exactly. Only things that are of legend or that an elder should be able to do."

"Like what?" the old man dug further.

"Astral projection, alchemy, and wish fulfillment to name a few," Master answered him.

"Are you in twilight when these spells are cast?"

"Gage's ass definitely puts me into twilight," Master said with a chuckle and then remembered that my father was listening, so he stopped and added, "No disrespect meant, Papa Gage." He turned to me and said, "Twilight is our word for a trance-like state."

Grandpa Earnest looked satisfied with that answer.

"So what does all this mean?" Dad asked, breaking the lull in the conversation.

I patted my father's hand and said, "It means that I will be taken care of from now on. It means that I can provide for you two and make your life more comfortable. It means that you can come visit me in Romania as often and for as long as you want starting today."

"You are not coming home?" he asked in disbelief.

"Dad, this man is my Master. I will live where he lives."

"But Romania is so far away."

"Not with magic, it's not. It will be just like us living next door to you," I said with a smile.

Dad looked at Master for a good minute and then asked me, "You have to do this because he rescued you?"

"No. I belong to him because I want to." I didn't know how much plainer to say it.

"It is my honor to protect and provide for him, Gerald," Master said with humility.

"You seem very capable of doing that," Dad agreed with him.

"He is. He is the coven Master for our trad," I told him.

Just then there was a knock on the front door. The doorbell rang a second later.

"Who could that be?" Dad asked as he made to stand.

"Let me," Master said as he made his way to the door. His large frame didn't seem to fit inside my childhood home.

Master opened the door and a voice said, "Good evening, sir. I'm Detective Combs from the police department and this is my partner, Detective Fedcheck."

"Yes?"

"We have information that the subject of a missing person's report has appeared here tonight."

"And that concerns you how?" my Master asked forcibly.

"Mister, I can tell from your accent that you are not from here and I know the homeowner personally, so please step aside and let us talk to him."

"By all means," Master said as he opened the screen door to let them inside.

What the fuck do they want and what is my Master going to do to them?

CHAPTER TWENTY-TWO

Texts between Sloven and the Coven Master of the Vrajitor Motorcycle Gang sent on the night of April fourteenth, 2019.

Sloven, how are things at home?
All is good, Master. How are things with you and Dart?
We are progressing and will go to see his father tonight.
Best of luck, Master
Thx. How did the pick-up of the prisoners go by the police?
It went well, Master. We did erasing spells on all of the kidnappers' minds.
It is a tricky spell to erase the memory of us but leave the memory of the punishment.
It is and the men were grateful that you allowed them to perform it, Master.
Many of them told me to thank you.
They are good men.
Yes, they are.
I am fortunate to have you as my second, Sloven.
You are a great man.
LOL. Does Dart have your phone, Master?
Seriously though, I appreciate your kind words.

The police detectives scrutinized each one of us as they walked inside the house. "You are Gage?" the one in charge asked me when he saw the blue mark on the side of my face.

"I am. I am just reconnecting with my family. If you could give us a few days, I will be glad to give you a full report."

"I'm afraid that will not be possible," Combs told me. "We are to question you now and then we will have to take you and the big man in for evaluation."

"Evaluation? For what?" I challenged.

"You have been through something very traumatic," the other detective said.

"Yeah, which you can't even bring yourself to say. I was kidnapped, sold into the sex trade, imprisoned for four years, and this man rescued me," I said angrily while pointing at my Master. "And now for our troubles, you want to separate us from our family and evaluate us?" I was furious.

Out of the corner of my eye, I saw Master reach into one of the pockets of his fatigues. Unfortunately, so did one of the cops.

"Hold it right there," Fedcheck said, putting his hand on the handgrip of his gun.

"I just have a root in here that keeps stabbing me," Master said, as he slowly pulled two thin brown roots out of his pocket. They looked like miniature sweet potatoes. He held one out to Grandpa Ernest and said, "They are Arrowroot to be exact."

Grandpa Ernest took the root in the palm of his hand and pressed his other palm to it. Master did the same thing and both of them dropped their heads. I knew they were conjuring a spell but had no idea what kind.

"We don't want any trouble . . ." Combs started to say.

Suddenly, there was a crack and the two detectives froze in place.

"A freezing spell, brilliant!" Ernest said.

"How long will that last?" I asked as I watched my father stare open-mouthed at the cops. He stood and ran his hand in front of their faces with no effect.

"We both did the spell, so it probably will hold until we release it," Master informed me. He walked over and reached inside the jacket pocket of the detective's coat and pulled out some papers.

"They have been looking for you for a long time," my father told me.

"I figured."

"The police have been nice to me. I owe them and they have a right to know what happened to you."

I stared at my father's face in disbelief. "They want to take us away," I said firmly.

"They have the warrants to take us in," Master said, shaking the papers.

"We have to leave," I immediately said.

"No!" Dad cried.

"You can tell them the story after we are gone," I said evenly. "I will tell you my story now, and then Master and I will go."

"No," Dad said again, tears starting to well up in his eyes.

My Master grabbed me by the shoulder, sparks flying. "Gerald, you can speak with the police after we leave tonight. Tomorrow, you and Ernest will pack a bag. I will return to Romania with Gage and make sure he is safe. Then I will return for you two tomorrow morning. You shall have your reunion in my country where I can make sure that we are safe."

"I would love to go back to the home country again," Ernest said with a look of hopefulness on his face.

My Master stared at the old man. "Are you an elder, Ernest?"

"I am, and the Trad Historian. I think I can help you figure out what is going on with you two," he admitted.

"And I have some questions for you," Master said eagerly.

"Do this, Dad, and we can take our time catching up. You will love Romania," I said.

My father looked at me with puppy dog eyes and pleaded, "You won't stay with me, Gage?"

"No. I will go where my Master tells me to go. He will protect me and he will protect you as well." I was impressed with the conviction in my voice. Dad must have been also, because he soon agreed to the plan.

I spent my first day back in Romania with my father. He wanted to hear the whole story of the past four years, so I told him. It took a long time and there were a lot of tears. We took several walks into the woods and there were a lot of quiet moments while he processed what I told him. It was hard on both of us, but it made us stronger.

The next day, my father rested while Master and I had a session with Grandpa Ernest. He wanted to see our magic, so my Master gave me an extremely hard fuck while I sat on his lap. He tore me up a second time by fucking down into me from above while I was bent in half underneath him.

It was odd to have a person I knew so well watching us fuck, but I hardly noticed him once Master had me impaled on his long-thrusting dagger. Ernest was amazed at the metals and diamonds that our fucking produced but was shocked at the blue energy ring the most.

Once I had two loads of Master's cum deep in my guts, Master sat in a chair with me on his lap, still impaled. He moved me to the side so that both of us could look across the table at my grandfather's best friend.

"I wasn't sure what this was at first, because there were inconsistencies with the lore of our people and what I knew was happening here," the old warlock told us.

"Like what?" Master asked.

"Well, the chief one was a change in physical appearance,

but that was answered when you came back to the United States to get us, Roman. You had physically changed and now you are back to your old self again."

"Both Gage and I change when we are near each other," he said, like it was nothing.

"I see that now," Ernest said with a chuckle.

"So, what do you think is happening?" I asked, drawing a sideways glare from my Master.

"I think that your elementals have combined to form a giant directional," Ernest told the coven Master.

Master interpreted for me. "Elementals are like life forces and Ernest thinks ours have formed to create an uber force, so to speak."

"Yes," Ernest continued. "I am positive that when you two fuck that you infuse each other with positive magical energy."

"Master certainly infuses me with his seed over and over again," I said tongue-in-cheek, drawing a grunt from the big man below me.

"It is called *cunning fire*," Ernest said, ignoring my jab. "An awakened awareness or achieving a heightened union."

"Cunning fire?" Master said, suddenly leaning forward slightly. "I've heard old stories about it, but I didn't think it was a real thing."

"I think when you and Gage are ... engaged, that you both go within. The result is a sort of ritual consciousness or altered state which is perfect for spell-making."

I nodded, because I understood that altered state now after weeks with my Master.

"But only one of us is a warlock," Master said.

"Gage has magic in his blood."

"But the magic we do is extraordinary, unusual, and very difficult," Master told him.

The old warlock chuckled and said, "Yes, I see. I believe

that you both are spell weaving."

"Spell weaving?" Master asked, with a thoughtful tone to his voice.

"What is that?" I asked. "Master?"

Master explained, "It's when you cast two or more different but complementary spells."

Ernest's eyes shone with excitement. "It is very rare and can only produce the most difficult and unlikely spells of great importance."

"I've only heard of spell weaving being performed by one person before," Master said.

Ernest, quite unexpectedly, grinned like a fool.

"Who?" I asked, unable to contain my curiosity.

"Merlin," both of the warlocks said together.

"Merlin? From King Arthur?" I asked stupidly.

"King Arthur was not the hero of that legend, the warlock was," my Master corrected me. "His cock was one of legend, they say," he whispered in my ear, his beard tickling the side of my face.

"I'm going to go check on your father, Gage. I will keep him busy while you guys do your thing," Ernest said drolly.

"Thank you, Elder," Master told him as we watched my grandfather's best friend leave the cabin.

"Merlin, schmerlin," I said, laughing to Master now that we were alone. "He can't possibly have a better dick than the one planted inside me right now."

"Is that so?" Master asked.

"It's a fact. Let it become legend," I said happily.

"Maybe we should see what this legendary cock can do for you?" he growled.

"It has already done so much," I said, closing my eyes and lying my head back onto Master's shoulder. "It truly is a magic wand."

YOU MAY ALSO ENJOY THE FOLLOWING FROM EXTASY BOOKS INC:

Batting Cage
Crawford Rhine

Excerpt

The cage was large, for a cage. It had a hardwood floor and smooth bars. Smooth bars are a plus for a cage. You would be surprised how often you touch them when you are riding in a cage, like I was. I'm tall, over six feet and the cage actually allowed me to sit upright and I probably could squat, if I ever wanted to.

I had been travelling for what seemed like the better part of a day, so my best guess was that I was out West somewhere. Time was hard to tell because there was a heavy curtain over the cage that blotted out everything except for a rim of light at the bottom. It was hard to tell if the light was sunlight or artificial. I was grateful for the curtain since I was almost naked in the cage, wearing only a jockstrap. My eyes had become accustomed to the dark and I would occasionally hear voices, although I couldn't hear much of the conversations.

I did know that I had travelled by plane and now by truck of some sort. I could tell I was getting close to my destination, because I could hear the sounds of a city and noticed the stop and start of traffic. The air was hot, so that didn't help my guessing. It was summer, after all. I couldn't imagine having to be transported like this in cold weather. That would have been even more uncomfortable.

Then I was being unloaded by what sounded like a forklift. The familiar beeping when they went in reverse and the quick turns made me pretty sure I was right. I seemed to be going down a long hallway, bumping across doorways. Then a quick drop and I could hear cheering and male voices. I instantly felt nervous and thought I might throw up.

"Trent, what did you ask for?" asked a husky voice.

"I asked for an older, tall, white, smart, southern, professional, masculine, outgoing Servant with a happy personality," said the one that must be Trent. He clicked off these qualities like he had them memorized from a list.

"Why southern?" asked another voice.

"I want us to like the same foods, of course!" was Trent's response. He had a nice voice, even in timbre, deep and powerful. "Well, let's see how I did."

The curtain was pulled off and my body instantly took over. I rose to a squatting position on the balls of my feet with my legs spread in a V-shape, my arms on my upper legs and my head bowed. This position really exposed me, especially in this jockstrap with no back and a front that was basically a band with a basket of fabric suspended from it.

The room was silent, but I knew there were a lot of guys there. I could see we were indoors—the carpet was high quality and patterned in a red and white scheme. I could see the legs of a lot of wooden benches that looked like expensive furniture. I could also see the shoes and lower legs of the man I presumed was Trent.

He was wearing cleats and baseball pants, the kind that are white with a red pinstripe down the side. My mind was going a million miles an hour, and I guessed I was in the locker room of a baseball club. The cleats were dusty and there was dirt on the bottom of his white pants. His shoes were large, if I was guessing probably a size fourteen. His legs matched his feet in size, so it looked natural. I knew that he was sizing me up as well, and he had a much better view than I did.

I consider myself in pretty good shape, but squatting in that position was not comfortable and I could feel the strain in my legs. I had always had good leg muscles, even if I didn't go to the gym, ever. I guess this was just one of the reasons why Servants were usually much younger than me. I was already very tense, and now my twenty-nine-year-old muscles were letting me hear it. The silence and the wait were agonizing. I didn't know what was coming next or what to do when it came.

My thoughts were shattered by the view of a hand coming towards me through the bars. It was a big, beefy hand, and I could see the veins popping out on the back and running up his arm. He was beautifully tan and had blonde hair on his forearm. I had to fight the instinct to pull away from him, hard.

"Look at me." I felt his fingers under my chin at the same moment that he spoke. They were lifting my head up towards him. I kept my eyes down as my head raised but more and more of the scene was revealed to me as I went along. It was definitely a baseball locker room, the Los Angeles Angels, as a matter of fact. I was in Anaheim. There were probably ten other guys in the room standing in the background.

I didn't get a great look at him, but I could see that he was tall, even though he was squatting to look into the cage. His uniform hinted at a body that was very broad and muscled. When his fingers left my chin, I turned my eyes up to his face.

"Holy shit!" I thought to myself. It's Trent Parks. His face was boyishly round and he had that familiar sense of serenity about him that I had seen when watching him on TV. He was very handsome, and I was thrilled he was my Master. Our eyes locked onto each other, and I was held by his gaze.

"I am your Master, and I'm very glad that you are finally here. I want you to know that everything will be great and you have nothing to worry about." The speech was stilted like he had been practicing it, but I felt sincerity roll off of him and I felt myself relax inside. His voice was very reassuring, and I was hopeful that this first meeting was to be how he would treat me in the future.

"How was your trip?" he asked.

"It was in a cage . . . .Sir," I replied, pausing too long before the required title.

The room burst into laughter, and I feared that I had just blown it. I looked back into his eyes expecting to see anger, but instead his mouth was curled up in a small smile and his eyes were twinkling with delight. Once again, I was relieved and let myself breathe.

"We're going to have to find something to stuff in that mouth of yours later," Trent commented, more to his teammates than to me, but I definitely heard it and comprehended his meaning. "I will see you later at home after my game."

The curtain was being dropped around the cage now, and I heard Trent giving instructions to the handlers for them to deliver me to his house and that his Dad would be there to let them in. He also asked them to make sure I was comfortable and fed.

With the curtain closed the guys talked freely like I could not hear them. Or maybe, it didn't matter that I could hear them.

"Well, Trent. Did you like him?"

"Is he what you pictured? Sometimes they don't get it right."

"He looked right to me!" This was followed by laughter. "He's a big boy!"

Then Trent's voice again, "He seems to be exactly what I

wanted."

"He looks and sounds like he can give you a run for your money, Parks!"

"I hope so."

"What's the agreement that you made with The Service?"

"Standard. He works for a year and he can decide whether to continue for another year. If he does, he gets the whole payment, if he doesn't, he gets half."

I heard the forklift before I felt it underneath the floorboards of the cage and then we were moving. Being loaded back on the truck and heading to my new home.

ABOUT THE AUTHOR

This is Crawford's third book in his series, The Romanian Chronicles. The Mystic Master follows the releases of The Dark Master and The Re-animated Master. He was inspired by a summer trip to Romania and Russia where he completed four books.

Crawford has previously published eight books in the Master & Servant Series — Batting Cage, Gridiron Cage, Celluloid Cage, Hardwood Cage, Ice Cage, Country Cage, Comic-Lined Cage, and Rusty Cage. He looks forward to continuing to travel and publishing more books in each series.

www.ingramcontent.com/pod-product-compliance
Lightning Source LLC
Chambersburg PA
CBHW070816120626
46556CB00002B/522